NICE DAY FOR A FUNERAL

The only law New York private eye Glenn Bowman can rely on is the law of the jungle. Frankie Siccola was one of the tigers in that jungle. No sooner was he sewn in a blanket than the scavengers got the scent of rich pickings, and only a fool would have come between them. Bowman was that kind of fool, and if he'd denied himself the pleasure of watching them plant Siccola in Belleview Cemetery a lot of things wouldn't have happened to a lot of people.

HARTLEY HOWARD

NICE DAY FOR A FUNERAL

Complete and Unabridged

LINFORD
Leicester

First published in Great Britain in 1972

First Linford Edition
published 1998

Copyright © 1972 by Hartley Howard
All rights reserved

British Library CIP Data

Howard, Hartley, *1908–*
    Nice day for a funeral.—Large print ed.—
Linford mystery library
    1. Detective and mystery stories
    2. Large type books
    I. Title
    823.9'14 [F]

    ISBN 0–7089–5211–9

Published by
F. A. Thorpe (Publishing) Ltd.
Anstey, Leicestershire

Set by Words & Graphics Ltd.
Anstey, Leicestershire
Printed and bound in Great Britain by
T. J. International Ltd., Padstow, Cornwall

This book is printed on acid-free paper

Set ye Uriah in the forefront of the
  hottest battle,
and retire ye from him, that he may
  be smitten, and die . . .

The Second Book of Samuel,
        Chap. II, verse 15

1

THEY buried Frank Siccola eleven o'clock, Monday morning, October 29. No one spilled any tears over his coffin. When a man has been a sonovabitch all his life, the only difference when he dies is that he's a dead sonovabitch.

It wasn't much of a ceremony. With someone like Frankie the proceedings had to be short if not sweet. Last respects don't take long where there's no respect.

Captain Henderson showed up about the time they were planting Siccola in the hard frosty ground. I wasn't surprised to see a member of the Homicide Bureau at Frankie's going-away party. The law was still hunting his killer. This far they hadn't got very far.

Counting Henderson and me that made nine at the graveside. Only three of us played any active role: a sandy-haired parson who looked like he had no bones

1

in his face, and a couple of grave-diggers who straddled the neat rectangular hole while they lowered Siccola down among the dead men.

On opposite sides of the grave stood two opposite types of women. One was a sleek, fair chick with blue eyes and hair smooth and lustrous as gold leaf: the other stacked up real good without being flamboyant — a well-groomed brunette with a quiet taste in clothes. The blonde wore a little black hat as a sign of mourning.

I didn't know either of them. But I recognized Theo Prager with his dead pan and fishy eyes. He was a type all to himself. He walked soft and he reminded me of an animal, alert and watchful.

The last member of the funeral party was out of a different stable. He had a pleasant face — not good-looking, not ugly. His crewcut was something between brown and ginger, his nose a trifle puffy, his chin indented with a dimple that added a look of toughness.

I'd met Ed Killick a couple of times. We weren't buddies but we knew each other well enough to give a civil hello.

In days long past, the DA had offered me a job as one of his special investigators. For reasons good or bad I'd turned him down. So he'd given it to Ed Killick instead.

I wasn't told if Killick knew he'd been second choice and I didn't ask. In my business I had enough problems minding my own business.

While the ceremony lasted, Ed stayed well in the background. Henderson and I kept seven-eight yards away from the others.

They clustered round the grave as Frankie's one-room bungalow landed with a gentle bump six feet down . . . the linen straps rasped against the base of the coffin as they were withdrawn . . . the grave-diggers began shovelling lumps of clay into the hole.

In a fruity voice, the parson whined " . . . Earth to earth, ashes to ashes, dust to dust; in sure and certain hope . . . "

That first layer of dirt always makes a hollow thumping noise different from every other noise. Anybody but Siccola and I'd have felt same as I usually feel when somebody's put to bed with a shovel.

With Siccola I had too good a memory. There were too many things about him to allow room for compassion.

I guess it showed. Almost inaudibly, Henderson said, "You don't have to act so damned pleased."

Anyone could've guessed where he came from. He'd inherited his dark hatchet face from his Mohawk ancestors who'd roamed upper New York State in the long ago before my ancestors butchered them.

Maybe he didn't hold that against me. Maybe he hadn't yet got round to it. We'd disagreed over most other things.

I said, "I act pleased because I am pleased. I've been looking forward to the day they threw dirt in Siccola's face."

"Never thought you were the type to let a hoodlum get under your skin," Henderson said.

"Ordinarily I don't. But in Frankie's case I made an exception. I hated his guts."

"So with you it's a nice day for a funeral . . . eh?"

"That's right. Now I'm satisfied. Now at last I've seen Frank Siccola wearing his pine overcoat."

Henderson felt in his pocket, brought out a matchstick and looked at it. Then he changed his mind.

When he'd put the match away, he asked, "Why are you so glad somebody put a .45 slug between Siccola's ears?"

"You wouldn't be interested," I said. "It all happened way back when."

The grave was nearly filled. I could see Theo Prager watching us. Ed Killick was watching Prager.

The two women were standing with their heads bowed while the parson mumbled the kind of stuff parsons always say at a time like that. They talk as if death confers a sort of sanctity.

Henderson half-turned towards me. With that old scalping look in his eyes, he said, "Never mind how long ago it was. I majored in history. Why did you hate Frank Siccola's guts?"

"Somebody in his organization rubbed

5

out a friend of mine," I said. "Whether Frank did it in person or it was done on his orders makes me no difference. Frank killed him — and got away with it."

"If you couldn't prove he was involved — "

"Nobody could ever prove Siccola was involved in anything. You ought to know that."

"Sure. But it got so's people blamed him for most things . . . even when he wasn't responsible."

"In this affair he was responsible, all right. I know."

With a quick look in Prager's direction, Henderson said, "Bearing a grudge for any length of time isn't healthy."

His dusky glistening face seemed to be asking a question he wasn't prepared to put into words. I'd seen that old predatory expression more than once in the past.

I said, "What's that supposed to mean?"

"Well, I could ask you if you've ever owned a .45 automatic."

"That's only half a question."

6

"Don't let it worry you. Just see you give me a whole answer."

"Then come straight out with it and ask me if I killed Frank Siccola."

"All right." Henderson shrugged as though he didn't care either way. "Did you?"

"If I had I'd be a dope to admit it," I said.

"What kind of answer is that?"

"The best you're going to get. I resent being suspected of murder — even the murder of a heel like Siccola."

By that time the grave was a long mound of lumpy clay. As the two shovel bums scooped up the last of the dirt, I added, "To keep the record straight I've got an alibi for the night Frankie was shot to death in that hotel room. When he departed this life I was making my usual weekly contribution to the same bunch of poker players I've been supporting for years."

In an unmoved voice, Henderson said, "I'm not interested in your alibi. I only wanted yes or no — not an oration. Get off your soapbox."

7

Guess our voices must've carried. The parson turned and peered at us with disapproval on his boneless face. Then he stepped back, nodded to Prager and the two women, and waved an open hand towards three wreaths lying on the grass verge.

The blonde chick had spent money regardless. Her floral tribute needed four hands to support it.

She and the parson carried it to the head of the grave and placed it reverently close to the headstone. Then she stood for a moment with her head bent as though in prayer before she moved away.

After that it was the brunette's turn. Her wreath was a simple affair. She laid it on the mound of clay just above the spot where I reckoned Frankie's head would be lying.

The whole performance took about five seconds. She didn't loiter to do any praying.

As she went back to the spot where she'd been standing a cold wind momentarily drifted through the cemetery and sent dead leaves rustling here and there.

Two of them came to rest right side up on the newly-filled grave with their tips curled inwards like yellow shrivelled hands reaching out from the earth.

Last of all Theo Prager went through the same routine. I reckoned he'd bought his wreath in a bargain basement.

He didn't waste any time praying, either. After a brief glance at the headstone he straightened up and went off along the concrete walk between the two long rows of graves. He moved like a cat — soft-footed and alert.

Prager had a reputation he'd earned before he got to be Siccola's top hand. He hadn't become any more human since then.

If Antonius had known Frank Siccola he wouldn't have said what he did or else he'd have changed it somewhat. But he'd only known Caesar — not Siccola.

" . . . *The evil that men do lives after them, the good is oft interred with their bones* . . . "

Nothing good shared Frankie's hole in the ground. But one thing was for sure — Theo Prager stood for the evil that lived on.

There was always a market for his sort of talents. New York rackets being what they were I didn't think he'd be out of work now his boss was out of circulation.

With the parson's hand cupped under her elbow, the slick blonde turned from the graveside and walked at a slow pace back towards the church. The way she acted she could've modelled for a widow desolate with grief as she left her beloved husband in his last resting place.

It was a good act. Pity I'd been around too long to fall for it. With her looks and Siccola's money, I reckoned she'd be sharing another man's bed before the worms joined Frankie in his.

When she and the parson were half-way down the paved walk, Ed Killick followed. He hadn't given Henderson and me even a hello. Maybe he thought we shouldn't treat a funeral as a social occasion.

After he'd gone that left three of us. The nice-looking brunette hadn't moved from the spot opposite where we were standing. She'd never once looked at anybody except the late Mister Siccola's widow.

Under his breath, Henderson murmured, "Wonder why she wants to stick around? The circus is over."

"Who is she?"

"Frank's ex. Never expected she'd show up today."

"Maybe it was for old times' sake," I said.

"You must be joking. Ever heard how Siccola treated his women?"

"I've heard," I said. "All the same, she might still have a soft spot for him."

"If she has it's in her head. Of course you can never be sure why a woman does anything."

"True — if not very profound."

The brunette glanced across at me and then went back to her contemplation of the headstone. She didn't seem to feel the cold of the frozen ground through her chic shoes.

I said, "I may be wrong but I've an

11

idea she'd like to be alone to enjoy her grief."

Henderson brought out a matchstick, put it between his teeth and began chewing the end thoughtfully. He had square white teeth that stood out against the dusky sheen of his face.

When he'd manœuvred the match to the other side of his mouth, he said, "Enjoy is as good a word as any. If Siccola could read Miss Diane Russell's thoughts right now I guess he'd turn over in his grave. You got transport or do you want to share a prowl car?"

"Thanks for the offer," I said. "But it would do things to my reputation if I were seen in the company of a Homicide dick."

Henderson shrugged. In a clipped tone, he said, "Anything that was done to your reputation would be an improvement. So long . . ."

I watched him until he got to the far end of the paved walk. After he'd gone out of sight that left Diane Russell and me.

She didn't look up as I went nearer.

Even when there was only the width of the grave between us she still acted like I wasn't there.

Not that I had any wish for conversation with Frankie's ex-wife. Nothing about him concerned me any more. My interest died same time he did.

Idle curiosity was all I felt as I studied the three wreaths. I wondered what wife, ex-wife and trigger man had found to say in farewell.

The first one had a card that said: *To my darling Frankie with undying love. Connie.*

On the middle one the message was brief and to the point: *Goodbye, Frankie.* It was signed *Theo.*

And the third wreath merely said: *From Diane.*

Taken all together they made a kind of pattern. I reckoned there wasn't much more they could say. Between them they just about summed up the life and death of Frank Siccola.

While I was thinking about it I felt Diane Russell's eyes on me. When I gave her an up-from-under look, she said, "You're Bowman, aren't you?"

It wasn't a question so it didn't need an answer. I just went on looking at her.

She was real nice to look at. My guess was that Siccola had traded her for blonde Connie only because he'd fancied one of the latest models.

Her voice would've been attractive if she'd been in an attractive mood. It had a touch of hoar-frost in it as she asked, "What are you doing here?"

"That makes two of you," I said. "Is there a law against it?"

"Don't — " her tone dropped to zero level — "don't get smart. Why should you come to Siccola's funeral?"

"I'm like Frankie. I just came along for the ride."

"Funny man." She took a long breath. "Now let's have some sense."

"All right," I said. "If you must know I've been following his career with interest — a very personal interest. When I heard the news I wanted to make sure it wasn't just wishful thinking."

"Was that your only reason?"

"I didn't need any other. Fresh air

always does me good . . . and now they've dumped Frankie in a six-feet hole the air smells a damn sight fresher."

With her lower lip held between her small white teeth she gave me a long up, down and up again. Then she tossed me another question.

She asked, "Know who I am?"

"Yes. You're Diane Russell — the former Mrs Siccola."

"Who told you?"

"The guy you saw standing beside me while the sad rites were being performed. If you haven't already met him you soon will."

"Why?"

"He's Captain Henderson of Homicide. It's his detail that's investigating Siccola's death."

"Oh, so that's who he is. I wondered . . . "

"Wasting his time, in my opinion."

"What — " something that could've been surprise thawed the chill look on her face — "what makes you say that?"

I said, "Because it was a mercy killing — a mercy for the community. If they ever catch the party who did it I'll

15

recommend him for the Congressional Medal."

Her expression thawed a little more. She said, "Talking that way isn't clever."

"It isn't meant to be clever. It's how I feel."

"If you go around opening a big mouth people might think you were the one who killed him."

"They'd be wrong. I didn't. But it's already been suggested."

"I'm not surprised."

"Neither was I. Doesn't stop me feeling that the President should declare October 29 a national holiday."

Diane went into a huddle. When she surfaced again, she asked, "Why haven't we met before?"

It sounded like a romantic question but I reckoned it wasn't — not with us on either side of Siccola's grave. So I said, "Should we have met?"

"Well, I was his wife until eighteen months ago and I knew most of the people he had dealings with."

"Frankie and I never did any deal," I said.

"Then what did you have against him?"

"It's a long story. Anyway, whoever gave him a one-way ticket settled the score for me."

In a reflective voice, she said, "So now it's all over . . . m-m-m? He's dead and forgiven."

"No — just dead."

"But you'd rather not tell me why?"

"That's right," I said. "Does it matter?"

"It might — to me." There was something behind her eyes I couldn't read.

"All you need to know is that his death doesn't alter my opinion of him. He was a louse — with oak leaves. OK?"

Almost meekly, she said, "You forget I was once his wife."

"Common law or — " with Frankie separating us she couldn't use her nails on my face — "or with benefit of clergy?"

She wasn't riled at that. She just said, "If it's anything to you we were married in church with all the trimmings . . . and we lived together nearly four years."

"If you could call it living," I said.

That vague something showed briefly

in her eyes again. She said, "I had everything that money could buy."

"So had Frankie."

Diane acted like her temper was beginning to fray. She said, "I'd have gone on taking the rough with the smooth . . . if I'd had the choice."

"But all good things come to an end," I said.

"That's what I learned the hard way . . . and just when I'd begun to think he'd grown out of his playboy habits."

There was no emotion in her voice. I guess she'd buried her feelings long before they buried Frankie.

While I was wondering why she wanted to tell me all this her mood changed. She looked suddenly older than her years.

It lasted only a moment. Then she added, "I still say everything could have worked out fine if he hadn't come across that drugstore blonde."

"Who was she?"

Diane bit on her lower lip again. To give herself time to think she walked slowly round behind the headstone and waited until I joined her. I could almost have imagined she didn't want Frankie to hear.

In a tone that could've burned holes in the grass verge, she said, "When he met that cheap tramp in Hollywood she was nobody — a hash slinger called Connie Munroe. Worked in a quick-lunch. Because she'd played bit parts a couple of times she talked like she'd been a film star."

"Must've had what it takes," I said.

"Oh, sure . . . and she doesn't mind who takes it. She's slept in more beds than the first Queen Elizabeth."

"Some good friend should've told Frankie . . . if he'd had a friend."

"Wouldn't have made any difference. Soon's she got her hooks in him, I was out."

"How?"

"He divorced me."

"You mean you divorced him."

Diane said, "No, that's not the way he wanted it. I had to give him grounds for divorce."

"At a price," I said.

"Wrong — " she put her gloved hand

19

on top of the headstone and gripped it tightly like she had Siccola by the throat — "wrong again. He didn't pay a cent. The way he arranged things I couldn't refuse."

"What things?"

"Either I provided him with photos of me having fun with another guy or I got a faceful of acid."

She made it sound as though she was talking about the weather. Her eyes were as empty as her voice.

I looked down at the headstone with its lying inscription: *Deeply mourned by his many friends and associates. RIP.*

Nobody would've gambled a bent nickel that his name and age inscribed in the marble weren't as fake as everything else about him. The only kosher thing in his whole rotten life was the date of his death.

Once upon a time Diane might've been a nice girl. Four years with Frank Siccola would be enough to corrupt anybody. It wasn't for me to sit in judgment.

I said, "We all make mistakes. You paid for yours. Now you've got it out of your system. Siccola won't trouble you any more . . . and you can make a fresh start."

"Thanks — " her eyes were almost humble — "thanks for listening. I don't often let my back hair down . . . and I'm lucky I had someone like you around."

"Think nothing of it."

"No, I won't forget. You're the kind of guy who's easy to talk to."

"And cheaper than a psychiatrist," I said.

She smiled at that for the first time — a quick flashing smile that made her look real pretty. I told myself Frankie must've had wheels in the head when he swopped her for Connie Munroe.

Then the smile got lost. In a colourless tone, Diane said, "I must go now. Maybe we'll meet again some time."

"I'd like that," I said.

It didn't mean anything. I was just making the right noises so she could stage an exit.

When she'd gone a dozen yards she stoppcd and looked back. In the same drab voice, she said, "You were right.

He won't trouble me any more. I'm glad he's dead. But it's funny . . . "

"What is?"

"He treated me like — " she stumbled over the next word — "like a dog and yet, while he lived, there was only one guy in the world for me."

Her eyes were dry but she looked as though she was on the verge of tears. I said, "You're not giving me that stuff about the old magic . . . are you?"

"Call it anything you want. I know I must've been crazy. I've always known. But it didn't make any difference. He was something that got into my blood a long time ago. When you get bitten by that sort of bug there's no cure."

The inscription on the headstone made me feel like throwing up. *Deeply mourned . . . RIP.*

He was under six feet of clay in a wooden box with the lid screwed down. I knew it like I knew the date was Monday, October 29. I'd seen it with my own eyes. But all the same I'd have sworn he was laughing at me.

By the look on Diane's face she felt

same as I did. As a change from hating Frank Siccola I began to feel sorry for her.

"You're cured now," I said. "Someone gave Frankie the right treatment."

"I suppose — " her eyes travelled from me to the headstone and back to me again — "you think I should be grateful."

"What you should be is your own affair. It won't mend the hole in Siccola's head. He's gone for keeps."

With a bitter twist to her mouth, she said, "You won't understand. No man could. I can't even explain it to myself."

"Explain what?"

"The way I felt about Frankie. No matter how he treated me I never lost my sense of loyalty. Guess it was all onesided but that made no difference. If he'd got rid of that blonde tramp I'd have gone back to him. I always told myself the time would come when he'd need me."

There was nothing I could say so I didn't say it. Foolish questions mostly get foolish answers.

When she'd moistened her lips, Diane added, "It would've done, too. If he'd lived . . . "

She turned away and I only just managed to catch the rest. " . . . Whoever shot him didn't do me any favour. I hope he roasts in hell."

"If he does, they can keep each other company," I said.

2

FOR the rest of that day, Diane Russell kept coming between me and my thoughts. Not that I had much to think about. With me, business was so dead it should've been embalmed.

Around five o'clock I took my feet off the old scarred desk, stuffed the *New York Times* in the waste paper basket and got ready to shut up shop. If anything of interest had been going to happen it should already have happened.

There's a saying about a watched pot. Something similar applies to a telephone. Mine hadn't rung once since I got back from Belleview Cemetery.

A couple of minutes after five, it did. I had my coat on and I'd just got to the door when it went off like a four alarm fire bell.

The wire wasn't too good and I didn't recognize the voice at the other end. Then the mush cleared.

Diane Russell was saying, " . . . I can't hear you. Who is that?"

I said I could hear her OK, and she said that was better and there must be something wrong with my phone because she'd been trying to get me since ten minutes off five and I said I'd report it soon as we were through with our conversation.

After that, I said, "Now what can I do for you?"

"Maybe nothing, maybe a lot. Depends how you're fixed."

"To do what, Miss Russell?"

"Well, I'd like to hire you . . . if you're not too busy right now."

There's another saying that no man should cry poverty. Near enough the same thing is telling the world that business is lousy.

So I said, "For the right type of client I'm never too busy."

Guess she liked that. In a warmer voice, she said, "You shouldn't commit yourself until you hear what sort of job it is."

"I'll take a chance. Do you want to talk about it?"

26

"Not over the phone. I'd like to call at your office."

"When?"

"Soon as I can pick up a cab. I could be there in around twenty minutes . . . if that's all right with you."

"Sure," I said. "Come right over."

That's how it all started. Maybe it was my own fault. If I'd denied myself the pleasure of watching them plant Frank Siccola in Belleview Cemetery, a lot of things wouldn't have happened to a lot of people — including me.

Ever since I had to earn my own living it's always been the same: if only I'd done this, if only I hadn't done that. Could be that someone slipped up at my christening. Instead of using water, I reckon they must've sprinkled me with a shower of ifs.

★ ★ ★

It was close on five-thirty when she arrived. I saw her glance round my twelve-by-ten office before she sat down in the visitor's chair and I could guess what she was thinking. I'd seen that look often enough.

I said, "I'm a one-man business so all I need is a one-room shop. Instead of a computer I use my head. That way I charge less."

Her eyes shifted from me to my four-drawer file, rack of books, ancient safe, wall calendar, beat-up desk, empty correspondence trays and back to me again. Whatever opinion she had it didn't show on her pretty face.

She said, "I want to hire you — not your office. If what I've heard about you is correct you won't be spending much time here."

"What have you heard?"

"Well, they say you're honest, hard-working and reliable. You haven't been known to betray a client's trust or shake him down because you think he can afford to pay a fancy price. That's good enough for me."

"It should be good enough for anybody," I said. "Who are they?"

"My lawyer, for one. I called him after I left you this morning."

"How was it you recognized me at the cemetery?"

"Your photo was in the papers a few months ago. I remember thinking at the time if ever I needed a private investigator I'd contact you."

She crossed one leg over the other, tugged her skirt down so I wouldn't get the idea she'd done it for my benefit, and made sure her crocodile-leather purse was secure on her lap. I had a hunch she wouldn't mind any other ideas I might get. Just a hunch . . .

When she'd got herself nicely settled, I said, "Nothing like publicity for drumming up customers. Don't you want to know the rates I charge?"

"No, I don't think you'll bill me more than you've earned."

"Maybe not. But if it's a lengthy job it'll cost you."

With a slight widening of her eyes, she asked, "Are you worried in case I welsh?"

I said, "That should be my biggest worry. Now let's get down to business."

She went on looking at me with

lingering doubt in her warm brown eyes. At last, she said, "I know you won't break confidence once you've taken on the assignment . . . but what if you can't accept the job I'm asking you to do?"

"If I can't it must be illegal," I said.

"Oh, no, it's quite within the law. The only thing is that there's an element of risk . . . for you, I mean."

"What sort of risk?"

"You — " she hesitated while she thought of the right way to put it — "you might get hurt."

Some of her doubt began to rub off on me. I said, "Does that mean getting worked-over . . . or hurt real bad?"

By now Diane knew how to put it but she didn't know how I'd take it. When she'd made up her mind, she said in a small voice, "I may be wrong . . . "

"Supposing you're right?"

"If I am — " she shrugged — "somebody may try to kill you."

"Who?"

"That's what I want you to find out. Your job is to locate a certain party. If,

30

and when, you do we'll decide what steps to take."

"Providing I'm still around to take any kind of steps," I said. "From what I can gather, this party has no wish to be located. If I get too close he or she will make it his or her business to see I don't get any closer. That's the position, isn't it?"

Diane made a rueful mouth. She said, "Yes. I realize it's asking a lot — "

"As an understatement that's in a class by itself. Let's hear the rest of it."

"Not until — " she wasn't at all doubtful now — "until you promise not to repeat anything I tell you . . . if you refuse the job."

They say it was curiosity that killed the cat. I said, "OK. I promise. What has this party got that you want so badly?"

"Something worth a lot."

"Cash or kind?"

"Real money . . . or as good as."

Her eyes clung to my face as she added, "Big money."

"How much?"

Diane said, "Half a million dollars."

She gave me plenty of time to think about it. When I'd used up my allowance, she asked, "Well? What do you say?"

In this town there were plenty of bad numbers who'd dispose of a kibitzer for less than five hundred grand — a lot less. I had a feeling I'd better get out before I got in too deep.

Trouble was that Diane didn't make it easy for me. Before I could tell her it was no deal, she said, "On top of your fee you could earn yourself ten per cent of fifty thousand. That's a bonus of five thousand dollars — with a bit of luck."

I said, "Luck comes in two flavours — sweet and sour. But leaving that to one side, what happened to the half million?"

Maybe Diane reckoned she had only to play the fish a little longer and he'd be hooked. In a tempting voice, she said, "The Eastern Fidelity offered a reward of fifty thousand. I'm willing to cut you in for ten per cent of my ten per cent which is as fair — "

"Hold it," I said. "I'm a bit slow on the uptake. What was it the Eastern

Fidelity insured that was worth half a million bucks?"

"Diamonds . . . that's what. A parcel of cut stones."

"Who lost them?"

"Shoemaker Gem Corporation. Two-three months ago their vault was robbed by a gang who tunnelled from premises at the back and came up through the floor. It was in all the papers. You must've read about it."

I said, "Sure. They called them the gopher mob. The police got a tip-off that the head boy was a guy called Connolly who'd been known to work with an expert jelly-man — Mike Tew. A week after the heist took place, Tew was found dead somewhere upstate. The law is still hunting for Connolly. So far as is known he took off with the diamonds."

"So far as is known," Diane said.

With just a glimpse of her white even teeth showing, she sat looking at me long enough to let the thought sink in. Then she added, "I happen to know different."

"Which means it isn't Connolly you

want me to locate," I said.

"What makes you say that?"

"Well, if he hasn't got the parcel of diamonds — "

Diane's smile reached her wide brown eyes. She said, "Nobody's got them."

If she was trying to confuse me, she'd succeeded. I said, "The more you talk the less you say. As I read it the police have a theory that Connolly disposed of Tew to cut him out of his split. Since the diamonds haven't been recovered, Connolly must have them."

"Not now. The theory's all right if you don't take it too far. After he got rid of Tew he parted with the stones . . . maybe because of the risk that he might be picked up."

"So he hid them somewhere?"

"No. He handed them over to the real boss — the guy who'd financed the whole operation."

"And you know who he is?"

"Was," Diane said. "You were at his funeral this morning."

Several things were now becoming clearer . . . but they weren't the more important things. When I'd added up the score twice and arrived at the same total each time, I said, "Who told you all this?"

Her smile faded. She said, "Frankie. He called me the day before he was shot to death in that hotel."

"Why should he confide in you after the way he'd behaved?"

"Because when the heat was on he realized I was the only one he could trust."

"Took him a long time to see the light," I said. "What made him think his wife wasn't trustworthy?"

"That tramp? He said on the phone he wouldn't give her the chance to double-cross him again. He already suspected it was through her he had to skip town. Somebody had been singing to the DA's office and he could guess who."

"How much did the DA have on him?"

"Plenty. He'd had a writ to appear before a grand jury this week. That's why he was skipping town."

"I'd rate that the best laugh of the

year," I said. "Frankie ducked one rap and walked right into another. If you believe in the Hereafter he's now appearing before the real Grand Jury."

Diane didn't think it was all that funny. In a brusque voice, she said, "Well, now you know why he called me. I always knew he'd turn to me if ever the going got rough."

"What did he want you to do for him?"

"Collect the parcel of diamonds from a safe-deposit. He'd sent me his key by special delivery and I was to get a letter of authority the day after I received the key."

"And did you?"

"Only the key. That arrived Wednesday morning. The letter should've come on Thursday but I never got it. I understood why when I heard a news flash on the radio."

She opened her purse, looked inside and snapped it shut again. The way she acted there was nothing more to say.

I had a flock of questions waiting to be answered. First go off, I said, "The safe-deposit key and the letter of authority aren't much good without each other. Why didn't he send you both of them at the same time?"

"Your guess is as good as mine. I asked him the same thing and all I got was a never-you-mind."

"Then what?"

"Then nothing." She shrugged. "When I heard he'd been shot I guessed it hadn't been for the kicks. Whoever killed him must've taken the letter."

"That's if it ever existed," I said. "Frankie might not have written it yet when somebody put a slug in him."

Diane dismissed that idea with a long cold look. She asked, "What other motive was there for killing him?"

"It would take me a year to list them. I should have half as many good friends as he had enemies. Besides, they found an empty billfold on him. Except for some small change he didn't have a dollar . . . and he wouldn't have taken a runout powder without seeing he had ample travelling expenses."

She didn't go for that suggestion,

either. She said, "No ordinary stick-up man could've got near Frankie. Anyway, who knew he was there? He'd checked in under a phoney name."

I said, "Someone knew. The key was on the inside so could be Frankie unlocked the door. In the circumstances he wouldn't have done that for a stranger . . . would he?"

"How do I know?" She moved restlessly and fiddled with her purse. I reckoned she didn't love me for planting doubt in her mind.

"OK," I said. "Let's assume there was a letter of authority and his killer took it. If Frankie hadn't been given a hole in the head and you'd received the letter, what were you supposed to do?"

"Collect the package from the safe-deposit. He couldn't do it himself because he was scared he'd be picked up."

"Is that all?"

"Yes. When I'd handed him the diamonds he was going to get out of town fast."

"Just like that?"

Diane sat back and held her purse close

against her. In a tone that was just too off-hand, she said, "I don't know what you mean."

"Then you'd better take your business some place else," I said. "If you start off by stringing me along you'll play me for a real sucker before we're through."

"I've — " her nice brown eyes couldn't stare me out — "I've no idea what you're talking about. Everything I've told you is the truth."

"But only half the truth. Do you expect me to believe you'd do Frankie a great big favour for free?"

"I don't care what you believe. If you want to refuse the chance of earning yourself a piece of easy money that's your lookout. I've given you all the information — "

"Last time I was offered easy money I finished up earning it the hard way," I said.

"Depends on whether you can look out for yourself." She tried to sound tough but it wasn't a very good try.

"No, it depends on how much trust there is between me and my client. This far you've given me the run-around. So it's no dice, Miss Russell. You'll find the door right behind you. Careful how you go down the stairs."

She sat staring at me with that empty look in her eyes I'd seen once already. When she'd moistened her lips a couple of times, she said woodenly, "I'm sorry. It was stupid of me. I shouldn't have tried to hold out on you. Will you accept my apology?"

If she'd looked like the tail-end of a horse I might've told her to go fly a kite. But she was very pretty and appealing and kind of woebegone. She made me feel sorry, too.

So I said, "There's no harm in trying. Now we understand each other we can make a fresh start. What was Frankie going to do for you in return for what you were going to do for him?"

Diane took time out to think up a little lie in place of a big lie. Then she accepted the situation.

With a resigned shrug, she said, "He was going to take me with him. When I'd collected the package I had to make reservations on the next flight to Miami. From there we would have sailed to South America. He knew the owner of a ship who wouldn't ask too many questions."

Only a fool thinks he understands women. I said, "If the scheme hadn't turned sour you'd have gone off with Frankie in spite of what he'd done to you?"

She gave me another long look, her eyes hard and bright. I got the feeling again that she had no more tears to shed.

Without any expression, she said, "Yes . . . so help me. Like I told you this morning, he was something that had got into my blood. It wasn't a share of the diamonds I wanted — it was Frankie himself."

"But now you'll settle for the reward," I said.

She should've hated me. She should've got up and walked out. But she just sat looking through my head as though I wasn't there.

At last, she said in a brittle voice,

"Guess I was born to be hurt by every man I meet. Never saw you before this morning and yet you stick a knife in me like you enjoy doing it."

If I'd cared about my image I'd have told her she was wrong. But I didn't care. To me all she represented was gainful employment. Attractive or homely, it made no difference what she or any other woman thought of me.

I said, "We'd better deal with facts or we'll get nowhere. Fact number one is that you want to get your hands on the fifty-thousand-dollar reward."

"Well, why not? After all I've been through, wouldn't you say I was entitled to some compensation?"

"I'm not entitled to say what you're entitled to get. If Eastern Fidelity are willing to pay you fifty thousand dollars, that's OK by me. But you're a long way from collecting. Anyone could've taken that letter of authority."

"No, not anyone. It must've been somebody who knew Frankie was tied in with the theft from Shoemaker Gem Corporation."

"Maybe so. But who?"

Diane stared through me again. Then she said, "Who ever has the letter killed Frankie to get hold of it. Probably they reckoned on finding the safe-deposit key at the same time."

"Sure. That sticks out a mile. But who?"

"Someone pretty close to him."

"That narrows the field but still leaves us with a lot of possibles. Homicide have been working along those lines and they haven't come up with the answer yet."

"Homicide don't know about the safe-deposit letter. They think it was some enemy who shot him."

"Well, it sure was no friend," I said.

"But — " she drew in her mouth and leaned forward — "but Frankie may have thought it was."

"Meaning?"

"It cuts down the list to a handful of probables."

"A handful is too many. I reckon you have one particular person in mind."

She said, "Yes. Who is, or should be, closer to a man than his own wife?"

43

Guess I'd seen it coming. Justified or otherwise, she'd do her damnedest to make trouble for the blonde angelface who'd taken Frankie away from her.

I said, "According to what he told you on the phone he didn't trust Connie. Wasn't she the one he suspected of having sung to the DA?"

"Yes . . . and I think she did. By the time he got wise to her the damage was done — in more ways than he realized. Who was better placed than Connie to find out about the safe-deposit box and what it contained?"

"A hood called Prager," I said. "If not better, at least as well."

Diane thought about it. She took long enough to work her way right round the idea and come back to where she'd started.

Then she said doubtfully, "I hadn't considered him . . . but maybe you've got something there. The only thing is . . . " She lost herself in another thought.

"Is what?"

"Frankie trusted Theo Prager. He used to say Theo was his insurance."

"Maybe the policy ran out when Prager caught sight of five hundred grand in cracked ice."

"Could be." She still didn't like the idea but she was prepared to give it house-room until a brighter one came along.

I said, "Now we've got two nominees. Any more?"

"Well, Frankie always watched out for a guy called Polk — Herman Polk."

She studied me with her head slightly tilted before she asked, "Have you heard of him?"

"Too often," I said. "Herman's another rat who's clawed his way up from the sewer. Now he's climbed as high as the gutter where he belongs."

"You sound like you belonged in a pulpit. Polk's no friend of mine. I've never even met the guy. All I know is that he and Frank were on each other's black list. If it weren't for that letter of authority . . . " She got lost again.

"You'd put him at the top of the ballot," I said.

Diane nodded. She said, "If Polk

got wind of what was going on and someone gave him the tip that Frankie was hiding out at that hotel all on his own . . . "

A worried look came into her eyes. I knew what she was thinking.

"The someone could've been Connie," I said. "Would she be dumb enough to trust Herman Polk?"

"Just say dumb — period. She'd be dazzled by the thought of splitting half a million dollars straight down the middle. That stupid broad doesn't know Polk would drop her in the Hudson an hour after he got hold of the parcel of diamonds."

I said, "Don't lose any sleep over her. If Herman Polk has the letter and he finds out you have the key, I'd say your prospects aren't anything to write home about."

That shook Diane Russell right down to her dainty little puppies. She stared at me wide-eyed and as motionless as though she'd quit breathing.

After a long, long time she swallowed and swallowed again. Then she said huskily, "You wouldn't tell him . . . would you?"

"If I did, you could sue your lawyer. Didn't he give me a first-rate character?"

"Yes, I — " she made a poor attempt to smile — "I shouldn't have needed to ask. You're not a chiseller. You keep faith with a client."

"Don't give me the rush act," I said. "I haven't yet agreed to take you on as a client. From what you've told me your best bet is the police. That way both of us would have a chance of living longer."

The scared look went for a walk. She said, "I can't tell the police."

"Why not?"

"Because I'd get nothing out of it. I might even land in trouble for concealing evidence in a case of homicide."

I said, "Not much risk of that. You could do a deal with the law. Captain Henderson's detail would be grateful for the first solid lead they'd have had this far."

"But the deal wouldn't include any reward from Eastern Fidelity . . . would it?"

47

"Guess not."

Diane didn't have to waste time thinking about it. She asked, "What sort of advice is that? Do I need you to talk me out of forty-five thousand dollars?"

"Money isn't everything," I said.

"It's a damn' good substitute." She looked at me down her nose. "You've heard my proposition . . . so let's quit horsing around. I'm offering you a generous fee and a fat bonus. Do you accept it or don't you?"

Now it was my turn to do some figuring. It didn't take long when there could be only one answer. I'd be a squirrel-brain if I got myself mixed up in the affairs of the former Mrs Siccola — bonus or no bonus.

I said, "It's not what I'd call a square proposition. I take all the chances and you take the thick end of the purse."

"Does that mean no?" She didn't act like she was worried.

"It means I might be willing to negotiate."

In a flat voice, she said, "Well, I'm not.

I've been straight with you all along the line. I didn't have to explain there was a risk attached to the job, but in fairness to you, I did. Five thousand dollars is my limit. You won't squeeze another dime out of me."

If she'd given in and agreed to raise the ante I'd have guessed she wasn't on the level. But now I didn't doubt that the story she'd told me was substantially true. A bit of distortion or evasion here and there could be excused in somebody who'd slept with a crook like Frank Siccola.

Behind it all I knew she'd hung around after the funeral because she wanted to talk with me. She couldn't have known I'd be there but she'd grabbed the chance when she saw it. No one could blame her for that . . .

About then, she said, "You've run out of time. Is it a deal or not?"

Common sense gave me one very good reason why I should reject her offer. But one against five thousand didn't stand a chance.

I said, "It's a deal. Have you got the

safe-deposit key?"

She opened her purse and brought out a slim wad of bills. As she tossed them on to my desk, she said, "That's to seal our bargain. If you go on working for me I'll go on feeding the kitty."

They were 100-dollar bills — five of them. Maybe I should've asked her where she'd got the money. Maybe I was right to think it was none of my business. After all she might've salted away a nice little nest-egg while she was married to Frankie.

It was the kind of precaution any smart girl would think of — life being somewhat uncertain for those connected with the Siccolas of this world. And one thing for sure was that Diane Russell was a real smart girl.

When I'd slipped the five bills into an inside pocket she fished in her purse again. This time she came up with a small thick book I could've carried in an outside pocket. It looked like the sort of book I didn't think it could be.

But it was. As she pushed it across the desk I got a touch of nostalgia that took my mind back to places and people I'd known when the world was young.

I hadn't seen a bible in a long time. This one showed no signs of wear and I reckoned it had seldom been taken down from somebody's bookshelf.

Diane said, "Open it and turn to the Second Book of Samuel."

There was no sense in asking questions. The five hundred dollars in my pocket told me this was no gag.

As I flipped past Joshua . . . Judges . . . Ruth . . . and came to the First Book of Samuel, Diane added, "Page 333 is what you're after."

She got up and leaned over the desk and I caught a whiff of the subtle perfume she was wearing. It was the kind that went with a five hundred dollar retainer. What didn't go with either her or her perfume was a pocket bible. That had me running around in circles.

But not for long. When I turned over page 331 I saw all I needed to see.

The middle of page 333 had been cut out. So had the next fifty-sixty pages to form a small cavity in which lay a shining brass key. It bore no maker's name — just an indented number: *12E366*.

As a hiding place the cavity was real cute. Its walls were coated with some kind of adhesive that held the centre area of the pages together without binding the outer edges. The key itself was stuck to the bottom page.

Unless examined meticulously, the Bible would've looked like any other pocket Bible. Even if held by the spine and shaken it would still have retained the key safely in its hiding place.

Diane Russell asked, "Think anyone would've found it?"

Her eyes were laughing at me. I thought it was a pity she didn't smile more often.

I said, "Not unless they made a special search. Your idea?"

"No, that's how Frankie sent it. He told me I should leave it there until I got to the safe-deposit company . . . in case somebody happened to search my apartment. Sharp . . . wasn't he?"

"Yes." The hollow noise of clods falling on a coffin echoed in my head. "But not sharp enough. I don't think he was skipping the country because he'd had a writ to appear before the grand jury. That was just one reason, a pretty good reason, but not the only one. I've got a notion he could also have been double-crossing a certain party."

"Who?"

"Connolly — the guy everybody believes has Shoemaker's diamonds. As I see it, Connolly must've passed them over to Frankie before high-tailing it for the hills. If Connolly suspected he was going to be left with a half share in damn all . . . "

"He'd be real mad," Diane said.

Without any expression, she added, "Maybe it was Frankie's idea to get rid of Mike Tew after he'd served his purpose."

"And Connolly was the hatchet man. Having killed once he'd find it easier the second time."

"But how — " she shook her head — "how did Connolly discover that Frankie was planning to ditch him?"

I said, "A better question is how Connolly or anybody else got to know where Frankie was hiding out. Yet someone did. There's a block of marble in Belleview Cemetery to prove it."

Diane withdrew into the secret places of her mind and left me on the outside. I told myself she looked nice and she smelled nice and maybe once Upon a time she'd been nice. But that was long ago. Four years of life shared with Frank Siccola would've defiled a saint.

For Diane Russell there could be no road back. I reckoned that was kind of sad. Everybody's entitled to a second chance . . .

Then she said, "That makes four: Connie Munroe, Prager, Herman Polk . . . and now Connolly. One of them must have that letter of authority."

"And won't stop at anything to get hold of — " I stood the open Bible upright — "this. If you take my advice you won't carry it around."

With momentary fear in her eyes, she said, "I don't intend to have it anywhere near me. From here on in it's all yours . . . until you locate the party who's got that letter."

I said, "If I do, what then?"

"You persuade them to hand it over."

"What do I use as persuasion?"

"The threat that you'll tell Homicide there was only one way the letter could've been obtained — by killing Frankie Siccola."

"If I say that, I leave myself open to a charge of concealing evidence. I could get ninety-nine years."

In a naïve voice, Diane said, "It isn't evidence. It's just my little theory. Who says you have to believe it?"

She made her purse snug under one arm. As she offered her gloved hand to me, she asked, "Any more questions?"

"Just one. How do I get in touch with you?"

She gave me her address and phone number. Then she took back her hand, smiled a warm sweet smile and walked to the door.

Guess she knew darn well I was admiring her legs and the sway of her body with every step. Those half-dozen paces were a lesson in chorcography.

When she got to the door she glanced

back, smiled again and told me goodbye. She looked vaguely regretful as she went out.

After she'd gone I was left with five hundred dollars, a mutilated bible and the elusive fragrance of her perfume. Whatever she'd been, whatever she was, my office felt kind of empty.

So did I. It was always the same. I always met the wrong sort of woman when I was in the wrong sort of mood.

This time I could blame Frank Siccola. Not that it helped. Nothing ever helped at the fag end of the day.

My watch said it was close on six o'clock. Before I grabbed a bite to eat there were a couple of things I had to do.

I dug the safe-deposit key out of the cavity in the Bible and replaced it with a spare key to the lock on my flatlet door. A few spots of gum held the replacement secure.

Then I hid the Bible under some papers in a desk drawer that could be locked. To the underside of the same drawer I taped the safe-deposit key.

Now only one thing remained to be done. Before I locked the drawer I roused an old friend who'd been slumbering there while I idled away the long weeks of an Indian summer.

The Smith and Wesson had gathered a little dust. I wiped it over, checked the action and put a full clip in the butt. When I'd tucked the .38 in the waistband of my trousers I felt a whole lot better. Its hard pressure against my stomach always helped to keep the butterflies quiet.

I didn't know when I'd need it but it was comforting to think I'd know where it was when I did. Frankie's insurance had let him down. I meant to take darn good care mine didn't.

3

SIX o'clock I called Homicide. If Henderson hadn't yet gone wherever Henderson went when he was all through with the day's chores, he could give me the answers to some very pertinent questions. As a taxpayer I was entitled to those answers.

He hadn't gone. He asked, "How did you make out with the divorcee?"

I didn't fancy his tone. I said, "If that means what I think it means, you should mind your own interference."

It was stupid of me to take the bait. I knew that by the way he laughed.

When the phone had quit making yuk-yuk noises, he said, "You always were a sucker for a dame."

"Nobody invited your opinion."

"It's a free country. Did you think I couldn't guess why you wanted to hang around the cemetery?"

"My reasons are my business. If it's

all the same to — "

"Times must be grim if you have to make a play for Siccola's cast-off."

"OK," I said. "You've had your fun. Now do you mind giving me some information?"

"What kind of information?"

"If you'll put away your gag book I'll tell you. What was the name of that place where Frankie got a slug in the head?"

"Duffie's Hotel . . . lower end of Forsyth. Why?"

"Because it wasn't mentioned in the newspapers and I was curious."

"About what?"

I said, "If both of us ask questions, neither of us will get any answers. How long had he been stopping at Duffie's?"

"Twenty-four hours. Checked in Tuesday evening."

"Under what name?"

"Called himself Sullivan."

"Any baggage?"

"One grip. Like a list of its contents?"

"Not unless there was anything other than a change of clothing and stuff of that kind."

Henderson said, "No, only what you'd expect. And now it's my turn. Why the quiz?"

"I'm interested in the last hours of the late unlamented Frank Siccola."

"How interested?"

Maybe I could've stalled. Maybe I'd have been a fool if I had.

What gave me an out was my recollection of Diane Russell saying "*Whoever has the letter killed Frankie to get hold of it . . .* "

I said, "I've been hired to investigate the circumstances of his death."

"Who's hired you?"

"That's a question I'm not obliged to answer."

"But you will . . . or you don't get any more information. I'd also remind you that getting your business mixed up in police business could put you out on a limb. So — give."

"My client is Miss Russell," I said.

The phone hummed and frizzled for ten seconds. Then Henderson asked, "Why should she care who put a hole in Siccola's head?"

"Why not?"

"Because he divorced her. I heard tell it was rigged . . . but all the same he ditched her without a cent."

"What you heard might be true. But it doesn't stop her carrying the torch for him."

The phone asked, "Who are you kidding?"

"I'm giving it to you straight," I said. "The lady told me herself."

"She's no lady. If you knew — "

"Don't tie Frankie's sins round her neck. She's not the first dopey dame to fall in love with the wrong guy."

"So you believe she's faithful unto death?"

"And beyond," I said.

Henderson thought that was comical. He said, "Harhar . . . Ever since Siccola tossed her out on her ear she's worshipped the ground that was coming to him. From here on in I'll bet she laughs herself to sleep."

"Before you start chucking your money away — "

"That brings me to the jackpot

question. What currency are you being paid in? Or is that a dirty answer?"

"You hope," I said. "But you're going to be disappointed. This is a strictly cash transaction. I've got a retainer in my pocket that would knock your eye out."

"M-m-m . . . you don't say?"

He sucked his teeth for a while. Then he asked, "What makes her think you can do better than the police department?"

"There's a good answer to that," I said. "But you'll have to figure it out for yourself. Modesty is the one — "

"Don't give me that fiddle-faddle! Has she told you something I don't know?"

If I wanted to go on operating in this town there was a price. I said, "Yes. She's convinced it was someone close to Frankie who sent him on a one-way ride."

"Such as who?"

"His wife, for one. Also Theo Prager. Also Herman Polk. Also Connolly who worked the gopher racket on Shoemaker Gem Corporation. They'll do for openers. Take your pick."

Henderson was in no hurry. There was

a long spell of frizzling and humming on the phone before he said, "The blonde tootsie is a possible. Prager, maybe. Herman Polk, doubtful. His feud with Siccola is too well known."

"That wouldn't worry Polk. He'd have an alibi you couldn't break. So would his gorillas."

"Sure. But he didn't have to get himself mixed up in something that looked like a gang killing. If he was behind it he must've known Siccola was skipping town and he wouldn't have left his body in the hotel room. If he'd dumped it in the river with a concrete foot-muff everybody was bound to think Frankie had taken a powder to dodge the grand jury."

"Something might've prevented them carting away the body."

"We're not talking the same language," Henderson said. "What I'm saying is that they'd have taken him alive. No need to slip him the bad news in the hotel."

"Have you had a chat with Herman Polk?"

"No, not yet. But we've leaned on

Connie and Prager."

"Who don't know nothing," I said.

"Well, you saw them yourself bearing their floral tributes."

"Doesn't mean a darn thing."

"Not in itself, maybe. But both of them did all right while Siccola was in charge of the organization. They might not do so good now he's been eliminated. As I see it they'd want to keep him fit and healthy."

"Somebody didn't," I said. "Could've been the same somebody who blew the whistle on him. Must've been strong stuff or he wouldn't have had a yen for far-off parts."

Henderson sucked his teeth again. He asked, "Why should this somebody fix it so Siccola would be arraigned before a grand jury and then knock him off?"

"Because he was going to skip the rap."

"In that case, why not call the DA's office and give them his room number at Duffie's Hotel?"

It was a logical question and I couldn't think of a logical answer. I said, "No bid.

Who put the finger on Siccola in the first place?"

"Your guess is as good as mine."

"Connie?"

"Same objection as before. He was her meal-ticket. Why should she want him sent to the pen?"

"I've no idea. But I'd sure like to know who fingered him."

"Don't ask me. I only became interested in Frank Siccola when he bled all over one of Duffie's carpets."

"How about asking Ed Killick? He'll know. He's the DA's fair-haired boy."

"Killick is dandruff to me," Henderson said. "You're kind of pally with the DA. Why don't you ask him yourself?"

"Because we only meet outside office hours. I never impose on social relationships."

"Bully for you." He sounded like his mind was some place else. "Let's talk about Jeff Connolly. How come you include him in your suspects?"

If I didn't throw Henderson a bone I'd end up giving him the whole joint. I said, "Siccola was behind that Shoe-maker

Gem heist. His money set it up."

Once again the phone made distant noises. Then Henderson asked, "Who told you?"

"Diane Russell."

"How does she know?"

There I got the feeling I had only to take one more step and I'd tread on a landmine. I said, "Who else should know any better? She'd been his wife."

"But not since he gave her the brush-off eighteen months ago. And the Shoemaker job took place in recent months. I can't see Frank Siccola feeding his ex with that sort of information. It would be like unfastening his collar and handing her a cut-throat razor."

Now the mine-field was behind me, I said, "How else would she know if he hadn't told her?"

"Who says she's telling the truth? You might believe she still kept a light in the window for him, but I don't."

"All right, so you don't. Now tell me why she should cook up a story like that."

"Because she's hated his guts from the

day he flung her out. She's just slinging mud, that's all."

As things now stood, Henderson could never say I'd held out on him. I said, "If you're right, she must've had a swell time this morning when they heaped six feet of mud on top of him."

"I am right," Henderson said. "One of these days Miss Russell may have to explain where she was on the night Frank Siccola was shot to death."

"Have it your own way. I just wonder why she gave me a fat retainer."

"Maybe — " the phone was laughing again — "maybe it's your stud fee."

His voice changed. He said, "Mind your step with that good-looking dame. I've got an idea she's trying to throw suspicion wherever it'll stick. Everybody had a motive — except her. Have you noticed that?"

It was a good thought. I said, "Not everybody. Her choice is Jeff Connolly."

"Why would he want to kill the guy who'd staked him to a half-million dollar heist?"

Maybe Diane was playing me for a

sucker. Maybe not. I'd soon find out. Right now I'd gone as far as duty demanded.

I said, "If and when I locate Jeff Connolly I'll give you the answer to that question."

* * *

The late Frank Siccola's number was listed in the book. After I'd had a quick meal I shut myself inside the pay station.

A little-girl voice asked me who I was. She didn't sound like Connie looked. When I'd told her my name she asked me to hold the wire.

After that everything was quiet at the other end. Then a different voice said, "This is Mrs Siccola. You want to speak with me?"

It wasn't a cultured voice but it was good enough for a hash slinger who'd married a two-timing fink. I said, "Not on the phone. I'd like a confidential chat between our two selves."

"What about?" Her accent didn't go

with her Riverside Drive address.

"Your husband's death in Duffie's Hotel."

"Why should I discuss that with a stranger? Who are you, anyway?"

"The name's Bowman — Glenn Bowman."

"Yes, I know that. My maid told me your name. I wanna know what business it is of yours and — "

"It's my business because I'm a private investigator," I said. "I've been hired to find the party who shot him. If you're not interested, just say so."

"Of course I'm interested! But you've chosen a bad day. In case you don't know it, my husband's funeral took place this morning."

Bad day or good day was a matter of opinion. I said, "I know it. I was there."

She said, "Oh . . . " It was a long flat sound like air escaping from a punctured balloon.

When she'd got her breath back, she asked, "Were you the man who was with Captain Henderson?"

I said, "Who else could I be? You've met him and I reckon you also know Killick of the DA's office. Your husband's triggerman, Prager, is almost a member of the family. So that leaves only the parson and me . . . and you couldn't mistake which was which."

Guess life with Frankie had got her out of the habit of quick thinking. Or maybe she'd been born without the equipment.

There was quite a pause before she said, "I don't like your manner."

"It's the only one I've got."

"That's not very funny."

"I didn't ring you to crack jokes. There's nothing comical about a guy with a headful of mashed brains."

The phone made a little sound that could've meant she was hurt, revolted or indignant. She said, "That's a horrible thing to say."

"Then don't say it. I'm being paid to uncover the truth about Frankie's death. You want to help — OK. You don't, I'll go talk with somebody else. The choice is yours."

"Who — " at last she'd got round to

the question she should've asked right at the start — "who's hired you?"

"We'll get down to cases when we can chat in private. Yes or no?"

Connie took a little more time because it was part of the act. Then she said, "All right. I'd like to hear what this is all about."

I said, "That goes for both of us . . ."

★ ★ ★

The house on Riverside Drive was very much like its palatial neighbours. A horseshoe driveway enclosing lawns dotted with flowerbeds stretched from sidewalk to colonial-style entrance.

There were lights in the ground-floor windows, a hanging lantern in the doorway. At eight peeyem on a frosty evening the place looked very inviting. I'd rather have slept there than in Duffie's flea box two streets from the Bowery.

My finger was still on the bell-push when the door opened. I reckoned she'd been instructed not to keep me waiting.

The maid with the little-girl voice was

71

a pudding-faced female who had fat legs and long dangling hair like a sheepdog. Short skirts should've been illegal for anyone with her legs. Two more and she'd have been able to support a billiard table in Regan's Poolroom.

Either domestic help was scarcer than nudists in a monastery or Connie had made sure she had no competition in her own home. My guess was that this roly-poly wouldn't have tempted Frankie if they'd been marooned on a desert island.

She didn't ask me for my hat and coat. She just led me across the entrance hall to a room on the right.

The door was half-open. She tapped on it with a pudgy hand, gave me a nod that shook strands of hair over her eyes and told me to go on in. When I was inside she pulled the door shut behind me.

It was an ornate room furnished with rich trimmings and poor taste. Someone had talked Siccola into buying too much of everything to show he could afford it.

Connie was different. She had all the right things in the right places. Maybe she couldn't recite geometry but when Frankie had gone shopping for a sleeping partner he hadn't been in the market for brains.

From where I stood everything on show was her own. And on her it looked good.

Smooth fair skin without a blemish . . . eyes as blue as the Pacific . . . hair like shining gold . . . With her looks she didn't need a college education.

The way she studied me down and up again she didn't need my company, either. When I told her good evening, she said, "I've been thinking."

That was good for a laugh any time. I said, "Better be careful or you'll do yourself a damage. Just give me the right answers to the right questions and I'll do all the thinking for both of us."

She clasped her hands round a knee that was a work of art. With her head tilted so she could look at me sideways, she said, "You got a big mouth. If Frankie was here he'd break you in itsy-bitsy pieces."

I said, "Frankie's in Belleview Cemetery

and that's where he's going to stop. Quit talking like a dumb broad or you'll make me sorry I came."

"If I tell Theo you insulted me — " she began swinging her lovely leg to and fro — "you will be sorry. Theo says I don't need to be scared of nothing while he's around."

"Sounds like he's fallen for you."

"Not the way you mean. He respects me as a person. No strings."

"That'll be the day," I said.

She let go of her knee, leaned back and linked both hands behind her head. It improved her visible assets.

In a tough voice, she said, "Guys like you are all the same. Only one thing on your mind. Want me to tell you something?"

"If I didn't I wouldn't be here."

"You talk in riddles." Her eyes were momentarily confused. "But whatever you're thinking you're wrong. I'm all through with that. From here on in a man is something in pants that opens the door so I can go out or come in."

"No kidding?"

"Not — " she drew in her full soft mouth — "not any more. The night I heard Frankie was never coming home again. I slung his pillow outa my bed. Now I sleep nights. And that's how it's gonna be. I've had enough of you-know-what to last me until I'm too old to be asked."

"Why tell me? All I want is information."

"In a pig's ear! You're looking at me same as all the other guys I've ever met. Well, I own me now. Frankie was the last."

"Very touching. Are you giving up the pleasures of the flesh because you're faithful to his memory?"

Connie chewed over the question as though she suspected a catch somewhere. Then she said, "Call it what you like."

I said, "I'd call it a load of hokum. Next time you go to bed with a guy I reckon you'll wear a black nightdress to show you're in mourning."

With no change in her face or her voice, she asked, "You think I don't care 'cos he's dead?"

"What you don't care is no skin off

my nose. I've got more important things on my mind."

"But I wanna know."

Her hands slid down until they lay in her lap. As she got out of the chair and walked towards me she looked different. She didn't come too near — just near enough to let me see a kind of lost look in her wide blue eyes. Then she said, "You think I don't care."

"Does it matter what I think?"

"Yes . . . even if you have got a big shnook." She put her little finger between her teeth and bit on it while she went on staring at me.

"All right," I said. "Do you care?"

"Sure . . . sure I do." She seemed to be talking to herself. "Funny, isn't it?"

That lost look got to me. I said, "Depends if you were happy with him."

"Happy? I guess so."

Her eyes drifted away. When they came back to me, she added, "I don't ever remember being happy . . . not real happy. Life's kinda tough for a dame like me. Until I met Frankie I'd got to wishing I'd been born homely-looking so

I didn't have to wrestle with every guy on the make. Guess you don't believe that . . . do you?"

Now she'd gone all wistful. If it was an act, she should've been on Broadway.

I said, "I believe it."

"You do?"

"Yes. Why shouldn't I?"

"Gee, that's swell."

The way she smiled at me anybody would've thought I was Father Christmas. She said, "I'm beginning to think I was wrong about you."

"How come?"

"Well, you act hard-nosed but — " she shook her head — "you're not all that tough. Know what I mean?"

"I've heard it before," I said.

That pleased her, too. She asked, "You married or something?"

"Or nothing," I said.

"No, you're not the type to stop in one place." She studied me like she was trying to read the name on my shirt-collar. "Now what?"

It wasn't a question because she just ran straight on. She said, "You remind

77

me of Frankie . . . in a sort of way."

"Thanks," I said.

"D'you ever meet him?"

"Once or twice."

"How'd you get on?"

"We didn't."

Without any expression, she said, "I guessed that. He played rough. Always said he'd been reared in a hard school. You didn't last long if you let the other guy get the drop on you."

"That's the truth," I said. "He proved it last Wednesday night."

Maybe she didn't hear me. Maybe it was over her head.

She switched to a different track when she said, "I've been thinking . . . "

"And?"

"Funny how I can tell you things . . . isn't it?"

That made twice in one day. I said, "Could be I just happen to be around when you feel lonely."

"No, it's more than that. I think you'd treat a girl right if . . . " She shrugged away the rest.

"How did Frankie treat you?"

78

"OK . . . I guess. So long as he had his own way we got along fine. It wasn't easy at first but I soon learned how to please him."

There were things in the vivid blue of her eyes that made me hope Frank Siccola would roast for ten thousand years. The phantoms were still there when she added, "Who was I to complain? He paid the rent and bought me clothes and gave me nice presents on my birthday and saw I never went short of nothing. So it was up to me to look after him . . . wasn't it?"

She was asking because she really wanted to know. The plaintive note in her voice summed up her life during the past eighteen months.

I said, "You were too good for him."

"Honest?"

"Cross my heart."

"Oh, I'm sure glad you think so. It's been worrying me."

"All your worries are in Belleview Cemetery," I said. "Frankie won't trouble you any more. You should've got somebody to put a .45 slug in his

79

head a long time ago."

She wasn't shocked. She wasn't even surprised.

When she'd thought about it, she said, "I could never have done that. Any time he slapped me around I knew he didn't mean it 'cos he always bought me something nice. And after that everything would be fine."

"Until the next time," I said. "Didn't you ever think of leaving him?"

At that she was surprised. She said, "Where would I have gone? This was the kind of set-up half the dames I know would've given their back teeth for. I had it made."

"And now?"

Connie wasn't listening. Like she was talking to herself again, she said. "This house and all the stuff in it is mine. I'm gonna sell it and get out soon's it's proper. No sense in stirring up a load of gossip, is there?"

"No sense at all. Did Frankie leave any money?"

"A few dollars. The lawyer says he must've taken a fat wad with him when he went to that hotel."

"But he only had some small change when they found him."

She put her little finger in her mouth again and nibbled it. Then she said, "Yeh, I reckon there was something funny about that . . . don't you?"

Her talk was baby-talk. She had the mind of a child with the morals of a whore.

I said, "Funny is right. Did you have any idea he had to get out fast because the heat was on?"

While she analysed the question she went back to her chair and sat down and stretched her legs out in front of her. It was all done very innocently. I didn't know whether she wanted me to look at her legs or not. What I did know was that Hollywood would've insured them for more than Shoemaker's diamonds.

Yet she'd only played bit parts . . . if Diane wasn't lying. I wondered how much sleeping around Connie had been made to do before she got even bit parts.

When she was relaxed and comfortable,

she said, "Guess you don't understand. Frankie never told me nothing about business. If he had some-place to go he just went off. Could be away two-three days. When he came back I didn't ask him where he'd been. Frankie wouldn't have liked that."

I told myself the law must've taken her all through this line of questioning. I'd get nowhere like they'd got nowhere. The only difference between us was that I wouldn't try to prove she'd pulled the trigger of a .45.

Under the light her hair rippled like molten gold as she shook her head at me. She said, "You think too much. It won't do you no good. If I'm not worried who shot Frankie, why should you give yourself a headache?"

"Because I'm being paid to find his killer," I said.

"Yeh, so you are." Her eyes were wide and innocent as a summer sky. "But you never told me who's putting up the money."

"His former wife," I said.

Connie tucked in her lovely legs and

sat up slowly. In a shocked voice, she said, "You must be kidding. I thought you were a regular guy but if you expect me to believe — "

"It's on the level. I've been hired by Diane Russell."

"But she'd have lit a barrel of gunpowder under Frankie. And she didn't like me, neither. What's it to her if he got rubbed out?"

"She says she still had that old feeling even after he divorced her."

Connie stared through while she bit on her finger again. At last, she said, "Well, whadaya know? There's no screwball like a screwy dame. And there was I thinking she went to his funeral 'cos it'd give her a big laugh."

I'd had the same thought. Either I was as dumb as Connie or Connie wasn't so dumb.

When I had no comment to make, she added, "Looks like Diane Russell wants to get square with somebody."

"You might say that," I said.

"But it won't show no dividend even supposing she does level the score."

"Miss Russell hasn't got your forgiving disposition."

"Where d'you get that forgiving stuff? It's just plain sense. Suppose somebody gets the rap for killing Frankie? What good will that do her?"

I said, "She thinks it's worth my fee."

"Yeh, that's what beats me. If you do your job you make a piece of change and some guy takes a trip up the river. But what does she get out of it?"

"It's her money," I said. "And, while we're on the subject, did a Jeff Connolly ever visit here?"

Connie pondered as though she had to reconnoitre the question. After she'd taken enough time to circle it twice, she said, "A Jeff something-or-other stopped by one night. Smooth-looking guy who didn't talk much. Frankie never introduced us but I reckon his name must've been Connolly."

"Why must it?"

"Well, Frankie called him Jeff. I heard that myself. And then there was those cheque stubs with the name Connolly on them. He didn't know any other Connolly so — "

"What cheque stubs?"

"The ones I found among Frankie's papers after they told me he was dead. He'd paid them out of his private account. It wasn't in his real name but I know Frankie's writing . . . and he once made a cheque out to me when he wanted some ready cash and I went to the bank and he'd signed the cheque with this different name. He told me that's how things were done in business."

"Monkey business," I said. "How many cheques had he drawn on this private account?"

"Two . . . maybe three."

"Can I see the stubs you're talking about?"

"No, I burned them."

"Why?"

"'Cos I don't like to get into no trouble . . . and Frankie said I wasn't ever to talk about the money he had in this bank or it would make trouble for him. With Frankie dead I reckoned I might be on the spot."

She looked at me brightly and asked, "It's reasonable, isn't it?"

I said, "From your point of view I guess it is. Didn't you remember reading about this guy Connolly in the papers a few months ago?"

Connie did some more pondering. Then she said, "I don't go much for reading. You get all the news and stuff on television . . . and it's easier to take in."

"That's for sure," I said. "What would you estimate the total amount was that Frankie paid this Jeff Connolly?"

"You — " she shook her head and made her sleek golden hair dance in the light again — "you got it wrong. The name on the cheques wasn't Jeff. It was some dame called Pamela."

Another woman in Siccola's life . . . I said, "You're sure the name was Pamela Connolly?"

"Sure I'm sure! I can read, can't I?"

"Of course. I just wondered if there could be any mistake, that's all."

"Then you can quit wondering. I told you already you think too much."

"Maybe you're right. Would you

happen to know where this Pamela Connolly lives?"

With a naïve look in her blue, blue eyes, Connie said, "Questions, nothing but questions. You're making me dizzy."

In the same tone, she went on, "The dame's got an apartment at Lakeland Towers. It's on Eighty-Fifth Street."

Something about her answer was just too pat. I said, "Did you get that from the cheque stubs as well?"

"No. There wasn't no address on them. I've known for ages where she lives."

"How?"

"Well, not because — " her naïve look widened to childlike innocence — "not because Frankie told me. I tailed him one night . . . that's how."

"Which means you'd suspected he was keeping another woman," I said.

"What else? When you live with a guy you can always tell."

"And after you'd satisfied yourself he was love-nesting?"

"Nothing. I don't know why I bothered. Frankie would've been real mad if he'd found out."

"Didn't you want to do something about it?"

"Do something?" Her innocence changed to bewilderment. "Why should I? If he got all he wanted from that chippy he'd leave me alone . . . so what did I have to gripe about?"

The simple logic of the simple mind . . . I said, "You should excuse me. It was a damnfool question. Now I must be on my way."

She got up and pushed back her hair in an elegant gesture. She asked, "Can't you stop a while?"

"Afraid not. I got things to do."

"What's the big rush? Let me fix you a drink. I like talking with you."

"It's been my pleasure," I said.

"Gee, you sure say the nicest things." She walked towards me, her lips parted in the innocent smile of a child. "How about coming around some time? We can talk about this and that and maybe have ourselves a laugh."

"One of these days," I said.

"Sure you wouldn't like a drink — " now she was close enough for me to see deep into the radiant blue of her eyes — "just a teeny-weeny drink to keep out the cold?"

"I'll take a rain-check . . . if you don't mind," I said.

She tilted back her head, put both hands behind her and held up her mouth. In a small voice, she said, "You're different from all the other guys. In case I don't see you again . . . kiss me goodbye like you were my friend."

Her breath was sweet, her lips were soft and clinging. But that's what it was — a kiss between friends. It lasted no longer than it would've taken me to count up to five.

When I drew away from her she sighed. Then her eyes slowly opened and she murmured, "That was real nice. I'll remember you, Glenn Bowman, I'll remember you when I've forgot what Frank Siccola looked like."

Guess that made me feel mean. She didn't know the thoughts I'd had while she was close enough for me to grab hold of her. I was glad she didn't know.

As I opened the door I looked back. She was still standing there, her arms behind her, in that innocent pose of a little girl.

But it was a different voice she used when she said, "That dill pickle is never around to see guests out like she's been told. I'm gonna get rid of her."

"This guest can see himself out," I said.

"Maybe . . . but I don't need her no more. It was all right while Frankie was alive but now she spoils the scenery."

"Not while you're around," I said.

It was a dumb thing to say. I knew that soon as it slipped out. But soon as is always too late.

She smiled like no one had ever smiled before. She said, "You think I'm pretty?"

"If I didn't I'd be walking with a white stick."

"And you promise you'll stop by to say hello and have a drink?"

"One of these days," I said.

"Make it — " Connie's smile was now as demure as the smile of a four-year-old — "make it one of these nights . . ."

4

I RODE a cab across town instead of calling first to let Pamela Connolly know she was about to get a visitor. What she didn't know couldn't do me any harm.

It was five minutes off nine when I got to Lakeland Towers. Four minutes off nine I'd already decided that either her husband or the late Frank Siccola — or both — had made generous provision for her. It took that kind of money to live in that kind of place.

Her apartment was on the fourth floor. Outside the elevator a shingle arrowed left: *Nos. 410 – 418*. I walked ankle-deep in carpet to apartment 412.

Under the numerals there was a discreet bell-button. It made a discreet droning noise when I leaned on it. After I'd waited a discreet length of time I leaned on it again . . . and again.

Another buzz got the same result. So

I took a ride for free down to the lobby and went out into Eighty-Fifth Street.

Nine o'clock was colder than eight o'clock. Since I'd gone visiting with Connie the frost had grown teeth. To keep my circulation going I took a smart walk to the intersection on First Avenue.

While I waited for a prowling hack to come along I added up the score. It wasn't very impressive. Frankie Siccola had two-timed everybody all his life and paid for it with his life when he made the mistake of two-timing himself.

That didn't tell me who even if I thought I knew why. And who was the party with the missing letter of authority . . . if Diane Russell was on the right track . . . if Diane Russell wasn't playing both ends against the middle with me as one of the ends.

Ten minutes after nine I picked up a cab and headed for home. My flatlet wasn't exactly the White House but it was warm and comfortable and I reckoned I could use an early night.

That idea lasted until I got to East Forty-Second. Then I asked myself why the yen for solitude. I could meditate just as well over a quiet glass of something to thaw the chill out of my bones.

So I stopped off at a little place near Grand Central where I knew nobody and nobody knew me. And there I killed the best part of half an hour thinking round and round in concentric circles that always brought me back to zero.

Ten o'clock I got home. It was still early enough for an early night. As I climbed the stairs to my two rooms on the second floor I pushed the life and death of Frank Siccola out of my mind. Tomorrow was another day. I'd had my money's worth out of this one.

It was only when I put my key in the lock that I got the idea this one wasn't over yet. The key wouldn't turn.

I soon found out why. The door wasn't locked.

That was discovery number one. Number two arrived when I pushed it open. My sitting-room light was on.

Number three had made himself comfortable in my best armchair. He didn't get up when I went inside and heeled the door shut.

I said, "If I'd known you were calling I'd have left a key under the mat."

Ed Killick stretched and yawned. With his fists at headheight like he was flexing his biceps, he said, "Don't let it worry you. A kid's money-box has a better lock than yours. I could've opened it with a toothpick."

"I'm not worried," I said. "Just curious. Is this a social call?"

He sat scratching his rusty crewcut while he stared through me lazily. He said, "Well, you might say it's half and half."

"What's the other half?"

"Official business."

"Not a good mix," I said.

"In this case — " he quit massaging his scalp — "I'm hoping to act as marriage broker. Of course, I could've asked you to drop in at the DA's office but it's better to handle things on a personal level . . . at this time."

"Better for whom?"

"Both of us. And I mean just that,

Bowman. You could be in deeper water than you think."

He sounded genuine and he looked honest. I knew he was known as a tough operator but he had a reputation for square dealing. If he wanted to proposition me I'd be a fool not to listen.

I said, "You make noises that don't make sense. Where do you get the idea that I think I'm in shallow water?"

His not-so-ugly-not-so-good-looking face crumpled in a frown. He said, "Do me a favour, Bowman. Don't horse around. You were at Siccola's funeral this morning. After the others — including me — had gone, you were seen having a heart-to-heart with his ex-wife, Diane Russell. Is that enough?"

"No. Who saw me?"

"If it makes any difference, one of the DA's bright young recruits."

"That means you've been keeping tabs on her."

Killick switched his frown to a grin. It suited him.

He said, "On her, on Frankie's cute

widow and on a hood called Prager . . . to name but a few."

"Since when?"

"Since the guy who'd given me a headache for a long time got himself a worse kind of headache when some kibitzer walked into his room at Duffie's Hotel with a .45."

"Why? You wanted to put Siccola away for the rest of his life. When he came to a sudden end so did your job."

"Oh, no, it didn't. Frankie had various interests with various people. If one of them had heard he was about to appear before a grand jury that one could've been scared he might talk."

In a flippant voice, Killick added, "I'd like to nail that one. He'd make a good replacement for Frank Siccola."

I said, "The one who did it could've been Theo Prager."

"Sure. Loyalty's all very well but, when the chips are down, a guy has to look out for himself — especially a guy of Prager's type. He'd sure hate the kind of publicity Siccola could've given him."

"But Frankie's wife and ex-wife had

nothing to be afraid of."

"Not so far as we know."

"If either of them got rid of him it wasn't because he might talk. They'd have a more personal reason."

"Very personal," Killick said. He sounded different.

"Suppose it was one of Frankie's women who did it?"

"Then I'll leave Homicide to pick up the pieces. But until the motive is established beyond doubt this case remains part of the DA's racket-busting programme."

I said, "Best of luck."

Ed Killick shed his air of flippancy. He said, "Luck isn't reliable. I'll settle for co-operation any time."

"If you're referring to me — "

"Who else? The way I heard it, you and Diane Russell had a lengthy chit-chat this morning. I'm here — semi-officially — to learn what it was all about."

"And if I say it was something confidential between Miss Russell and me?"

He put both hands over his mouth

to hide a yawn. When he'd stretched again, he said, "You should excuse me. I've been awake all day — and my day started at five ack emma."

"It's a hard life," I said.

"That's for a fact. Funny how nobody ever wants to bow out. I've often wondered how folks could sing that old hymn about a happy land. Remember it?"

"I haven't sung any hymns in a long time," I said.

"Oh, but you must know this one: There is a happy land far, far away . . . "

His voice was quite tuneful. By the look in his eyes he was thinking of days long ago.

Then he roused himself. With a crooked grin, he asked, "Do you suppose they've got a place in that happy land for Frank Siccola?"

"Depends how choosy the selection committee happens to be."

"Yeh, like in most things."

Without relaxing his grin, he added, "Goes for you, too."

"What does?"

"Making a choice between law enforcement and Miss Russell's confidences."

"That's an over-simplification," I said. "Have you any reason to believe she's done something wrong?"

"No . . . but what she told you may help me to put something right."

"And if I don't see it that way?"

Ed Killick looked at me with the corners of his mouth pulled down. I had a feeling he was trying to read my mind.

At last, he said, "You'll disappoint me — that's all. You rate pretty good in this town and I was hoping we might trade information. Still, I've been disappointed before . . . and I can't force you to open up."

"Suppose you could?"

He gave me a different look. Then he shrugged and said, "I wouldn't — not a guy like you. But don't forget there might come a time when you'll need me."

I said, "And if that time ever comes you'll pay me back in my own coin."

His homespun face creased in another

grin. He said, "Suppose we wait and see . . . huh?"

One thing I knew for sure. The choice was mine. I could hold out on him or I could tell him the half-truth that's worse than a lie.

But a square deal had to work both ways. If he levelled with me I couldn't give him a fast shuffle.

So I said, "Look. I'll tell you whatever I believe to be fact. Anything else I'd rather keep under my hat. You've probably got your own theories and you can get by without mine. OK?"

He eased himself out of my best arm-chair and did some limbering-up exercises while he went through his thought-reading routine again. Then he said, "Sounds up-and-up. I could use a few facts. But I'm kind of puzzled, all the same."

"What about?"

"Your change of mind. They say you've always been a loner . . . and I'd have laid better than evens you meant to keep Miss Russell's confidences to yourself."

"You'd have collected," I said.

"Except for what?"

"That crack of yours about a time coming when I might need you."

He made big eyes. He asked, "So?"

I said, "So this. I always ride a hunch. And I got a hunch the time has just about arrived. There's no future in trying to look two ways at once."

Killick nodded and went on nodding like one of those toy animals on the rear parcel shelf of a car. He said, "It's never too late to get wise."

"How about Frankie Siccola? If he hadn't left it too late he wouldn't have been planted in the bone orchard this morning."

"It couldn't have happened to a nicer guy," Killick said. "My only complaint is that it let him off the hook before he'd been made to sweat. That's one reason why I've got a bone to pick with the party who used that .45."

"Must've been somebody who knew Frankie was on the run," I said. "Could be the somebody who fingered him. Guess you've already thought of that."

"Till I got noises in the head." Ed

Killick scrubbed his crewcut irritably. "It figures . . . except for one thing."

"Such as?"

"Such as the canary's got an alibi. We had the place staked-out that night."

"Maybe your stake-out fell asleep on the job."

Killick thought that rated a sour grin. He said, "Uh-uh. Not a chance. Siccola got himself shot around nine-thirty . . . and I'd taken the swing shift Wednesday evening. So I was the stake-out."

"You must've expected that Frankie would try to hit back."

"Nothing surer. Soon's I heard he'd skipped I reckoned our informant could use some protection."

"How would Frankie know who'd put the finger on him?"

"Be your age!" Killick did another spell of limbering-up and then he asked, "How did he know the heat was on? Don't both things tie in together?"

As I saw it there could've been several explanations. And none of mine agreed with Killick's idea that Siccola must've had a line to the DA's office.

I said, "Mind telling me the name of your informant?"

Ed Killick put on a phoney look of embarrassment. He said, "You ought to know better than to ask me something like that. If I passed on hush-hush information the DA would have my hide."

"Who is there to tell him?"

"You'd be surprised how things slip out. Right now my boss is scratching around for the big mouth who tipped our hand to Siccola."

With a quick glance at his watch, Killick asked, "What did you and Diane Russell talk about?"

It was a straight question and I'd have liked to give him a straight answer. But Diane trusted me even if I didn't entirely trust her.

So I said, "Frankie Siccola . . . among other things."

"What other things?"

"The blonde tootsie who pushed her nose out."

"And?"

"And also Theo Prager and a guy

called Polk whom you've probably heard of."

Killick nodded again like one of those spring-necked animals in a car rear window. He said, "I've heard of Herman Polk. Why is Miss Russell interested in these assorted characters?"

"She has an idea one of them killed her ex-husband."

"Supposing one of them did? I'd have thought she'd prefer to let sleeping dogs lie . . . and Frankie sure was a low-down dog."

"You'd have thought wrong," I said. "In spite of the way he'd treated her she still had a thing about him and she doesn't want his killer to get away with it."

"Who says?"

"She does. And to prove it she's paying me good money to find the party who walked into Siccola's room at Duffie's Hotel waving a .45."

Ed Killick folded one hand in the other and squeezed until his knuckles cracked. What he had on his mind wasn't what came out of his mouth when he asked,

"How much is good money?"

"Depends on your standard of living," I said. "Me, I've got simple tastes."

He wasn't listening. After he'd cracked his knuckles some more, he said, "If you think she's on the level you must've come up the Mississippi in a barrel. Don't you know people wouldn't be surprised if she'd done it herself?"

"People are entitled to think what they like. I only know what she told me."

"And you believe her?"

"Until I've got proof she's stringing me along."

"Some guys — " he checked his watch again — "will do anything for money."

"Henderson put it another way," I said. "His remark was that I'd always been a sucker for a good-looking dame."

"You mean he knows you've been hired by Miss Russell?"

"Yes. We had a chat on the phone at six o'clock and I had to explain why I was interested in the last hours of Frank Siccola."

In an off-hand voice, Killick said,

"Sounds like you're pally with Captain Henderson."

"He'd get a big laugh out of that," I said. "He's got a morbid sense of humour."

The way Killick stared right through me I'd have laid square odds he wasn't listening again. When he came back to the here and now, he asked, "Did Diane Russell say anything about seeing her ex-husband recently?"

It was a relief to be able to tell the truth. I said, "To the best of my knowledge she never saw Frankie after he divorced her."

"Yet she went on feeling sentimental about him although she'd been tossed out on her ear?"

"That's what she says."

"And she's burned up with the desire to make somebody pay for his death?"

"Nothing surer," I said. "Her exact words were ' . . . Whoever shot him didn't do me any favour. I hope he roasts in hell.' If you'd been there you'd have known she meant it."

"What does she think you can do that

Homicide can't do better — and for free?"

"It's her own money," I said. "I tried putting in a word for the Homicide Bureau but she wouldn't go along with it. If I'd refused the assignment she'd have gone shopping some-place else."

"All because she wants to see justice done . . . eh?"

"Well, there's nothing wrong with that. If she — "

"There's everything wrong with it. She might've been the one who gunned Frankie down. Have you thought this could be her way of covering up?"

I could've told him I'd had that thought but the facts were against it. If Diane had killed Siccola she wouldn't have needed me to hunt for the letter of authority. She'd already have it.

She wouldn't have needed the reward, either. Half a million in cut gems would've been all hers. She had only to wait until the affair cooled off and then collect a parcel from the safe-deposit and go travelling in foreign parts.

107

No one would know she had the Shoemaker Corporation's diamonds. No one had known Frankie had them . . . except Jeff Connolly . . . if there was any truth in the story Frankie had told her . . . if there was any truth in the story she'd told me . . .

Meanwhile Killick was waiting for an answer. I said, "You're making it too complicated. Whether she hated Frankie like poison or he was still a flame that hadn't gone out makes me no difference. I'm as sure as can be that I wasn't hired as a cover-up."

If Ed Killick was satisfied he should've told his face. In his position I wouldn't have been satisfied, either.

But he didn't argue. He just stared at me solemnly while he hunched his shoulders a couple of times like they were stiff.

Then he said, "It's getting late and I've had a long day. Mind if I use your phone to call a taxi?"

I gave him the number of the nearest cab depot. When he'd hung up he studied me again long and thoughtfully.

At last he said, "I hope you know what you're doing."

"Meaning you think Miss Russell's taking me for a ride."

"No, not exactly that. You may not appreciate just how many rackets Frankie Siccola was mixed up in. Even if his death was strictly a family matter there are plenty of people in this town who won't be keen to have a guy like you turning over various damp rocks to see what crawls out. And they have their own way of dealing with snoopers."

That would've reminded me of Diane . . . except that I didn't need any reminding. I could hear her saying in a small voice " . . . *Somebody may try to kill you.*"

For a moment I was tempted to come clean with him. If I had, maybe it would've made no difference in the long run. When I went to Siccola's funeral the wheels were set in motion. They'd got out of control by the time Diane left my office.

I said, "Can you name anyone specific?"

Ed Killick gave me a wry grin. He

109

said, "The list is as long as your arm. And it wouldn't do you any good. If you took my advice you'd leave town before Herman Polk and his kind get to hear you're poking your nose into Siccola's affairs."

"How do I know they haven't heard it already?"

"If they have it'll be just too bad. You'll be stuck with Miss Diane Russell whether you like it or not. There's an old saying: He who rides the tiger can't get off."

With no trace of humour on his homely face, Killick added, "The advantage of running a one-man outfit is that you cut down on overheads. The disadvantage is that you've no one to ride shotgun for you."

"Thanks," I said. "Glad you stopped by. You've been a great source of comfort."

Down below in the street a car hooted twice. Killick said, "That'll be my taxi. If you should remember something you forgot to tell me, I'll be pleased to hear about it."

"There's nothing to tell," I said.

110

"Have it your own way."

He fastened his coat as he went to the door. When he was outside in the hallway he looked back at me and asked, "You got a gun?"

"Cleaned, oiled and fully loaded," I said.

"Good. I'm not a scaremonger but — " his eyes were serious — "from here on in you'd be wise not to go anywhere without it."

The cab hooted again. He gave me a parting nod and pulled the door shut.

I listened to his brisk footsteps recede along the hallway. As he trotted downstairs I turned the key in the lock and propped a chair under the knob. Then I walked over to the living-room window.

All this time I had an uneasy feeling about Ed Killick. He'd been so busy dishing out advice to me he might've forgotten to look out for himself. We weren't buddies but he'd talked fair and I didn't want anything to happen to him.

In the ordinary way he was safe enough. Even the biggest mobster knew it paid no dividends to get tough with a member of the DA's staff. Another one merely took his place. And the law never let up.

But somebody might mistake Killick for me. If the word had got around . . .

It was too soon. I kept telling myself they'd be in no hurry. Time enough when I'd become a nuisance.

There I thought about Connie. Maybe Theo Prager had heard I'd visited with her. Maybe she'd told him. Maybe she wasn't as dumb as she made out.

Down below I could see the cab. It was parked at the kerb ten yards along the street, its exhaust vapour steaming red around one of the tail lamps in the frosty night air.

While I watched, Ed Killick came out. The cab door opened as he crossed the sidewalk and climbed inside. With its exhaust spiralling crimson smoke the cab began to roll.

On the other side of the street a young couple went by, their arms round each other. They stopped and kissed as the cab went out of sight. There was no one else to be seen.

Somewhere in the distance the cab

shifted into high. I stood listening until its motor became part of the murmur of far-off traffic. After that I reckoned I'd scared myself for no reason at all.

When the teenagers had gone, the overhead lights shone down on an empty street. I felt kind of empty as well. The whole performance had been for nothing.

I'd known it was too soon to expect trouble . . . if there was ever going to be any trouble. Things would warm up only if someone talked about the parcel of cut stones that Frankie Siccola had stashed away in a safe-deposit.

But Diane wouldn't talk. And I had no yen to publicize the job I'd been hired to do. No one knew a parcel worth half a million dollars was waiting to be picked up — no one but Diane and me.

That was when I remembered Jeff Connolly. If he had come back to give Frank Siccola the pay-off he had that letter of authority . . . but it was of no value without the safe-deposit key. So, wherever he was, he would have to come back again.

As I saw it he couldn't know who had the key. As I saw it he had no way of finding out. But his options were limited. Only a few people had been close to Frankie Siccola: his wife, his ex-wife and a cold-blooded animal called Theo Prager.

My choice was no choice. If Diane Russell and Connie were on the level, Jeff Connolly was a laydown. He'd been robbed of both his wife and his slice of half a million dollars. That gave him two darn good motives for calling on Frank Siccola with a .45.

While I was cleaning my teeth and getting ready for bed I did some more thinking about Connolly. The way it all added up I wouldn't need to find him: he'd come looking for me . . . if he knew I'd been hired by Diane Russell . . . if he knew I'd dropped in at the house on Riverside Drive . . .

There I quit chasing imponderables round and round inside my head. It wasn't getting me anywhere. What I needed was a good night's rest. Problems always deflated when I'd slept on them.

I turned down the bedclothes, set the alarm for seven a.m. and stuffed my Smith and Wesson under the pillow. The prospect of eight hours' sleep was very inviting.

Before I switched off the living-room light I checked the door to the hallway. I knew it was locked and bolted but something compelled me to make sure. The same something warned me it wouldn't take much for my nerves to get out of hand.

Through a gap in the drapes I looked down at the deserted street. Maybe it was because I was tired, maybe it was because I'd let Ed Killick throw a scare into me, but I had that empty feeling again — the feeling that I was all alone in a hostile world.

Nobody cared a damn if I went to bed and never woke up. I had no family and few friends. My weekly poker game would get by without me. They'd find someone to take my place. There was always somebody around who could fill a vacant chair.

That thought jelled in my mind as I

115

stepped back to pull the drapes together. I was reaching up with both hands when I saw a hole appear in the glass two-three inches to the right of my head.

It was a small round hole with cracks radiating from it in the shape of a star. One crack spread farther than the others like a line of silver travelling almost to the window frame. It seemed to lengthen very slowly.

Then I heard something plop into the wall across the living-room. In that same fraction of time there was a sound like the bursting of a paper bag in the street below.

5

AS the noise of that miniature explosion echoed from the side-walk below my window there were two things I knew. One was that some sonovabitch in a doorway across the street had taken a shot at me. The other was that I made a darn good target standing there with the light behind me.

I'd set myself up like one of those figures in a shooting gallery. Diane had warned me. Ed Killick had warned me. My own instincts had warned me. If I hadn't had a luckier break than I deserved . . .

All that took no longer than the interval between the gunshot and the echo. Before the next moment arrived I'd thrown myself to the floor. And there I lay until my heart quit pounding like a drum.

Down below in the street running footsteps crossed the pavement — light footsteps that could've been made by either a man or a woman. When I reckoned they were near enough to be almost beneath my window they stopped . . . and then walked on so quietly they were barely audible.

I had no means of knowing when they had or if they had gone. To risk taking a peek out of the window would've been just plain crazy. I couldn't see anyone immediately below my flatlet . . . and there might've been two of them. The one with the gun might still be lurking in a doorway across the street.

A couple of minutes passed. Random sounds in the distance were all I could hear. No one soft-footed up the stairs, no one approached my door. After another minute it began to look as though the party outside had decided to call it a night.

Somewhere somebody was feeling pleased at a job well done. I'd been disposed of with a slug in the head — like Frankie Siccola. Two nuisances eliminated in the same way . . .

That's what I thought to myself while I was lying there without making a move.

If I waited long enough somebody would think I was dead . . . but might want to be quite sure . . . and might come calling when my living-room light was still on long after bedtime. Anyway, that's what I thought.

A car came along the street — not fast, not slow. I had a feeling it slackened speed before it reached my apartment block but that could've been imagination. It didn't stop.

After that I waited maybe another minute. Then I made like a crab into the bedroom.

With the Smith and Wesson pressing against my stomach I felt a whole lot easier in mind. Outside in the hallway and down below in the street everything was still nice and quiet. I got the idea my long day was over at last.

But I could've been wrong. And the second attempt might not fail.

So I sidled into the living-room, kept well back from the window and worked my way round the wall to the spot where something had gone plop. From there I couldn't see the street below. The odds were I couldn't be seen, either.

There was a shapeless hole in the plaster just about where wall and ceiling met. I stood on a chair and used a small screwdriver to dig out the shell.

It was a battered but still recognizable slug from a .45. I'd had a hunch it would be. The proof that I'd been right didn't give me any satisfaction.

My watch said the time was close on eleven o'clock. I unbolted the door to the hallway, removed the chair from under the knob and turned it wrong way round. Then I sat down astride the chair and used its back-rest as a prop for the Smith and Wesson.

Time moped along. After an hour went by I found it was only eleven-fifteen. It took nearly as long again before the hands of my watch moved on to eleven-twenty.

A little later I guess I must've dozed off. When I woke up my head was pillowed on my arms but I hadn't let go of the .38.

It was the ringing of the phone that had roused me. I sat listening to the shrill noise of the bell prodding me to answer — listening and wondering what the caller would do when there was no reply. If I'd guessed right I didn't need to wonder.

And still the persistent ringing of the bell went on. I hadn't any doubt now. Only one person could be ringing my number. No one I knew would call me at that hour of the night, no one I knew would refuse to take no for an answer.

At long last the clamour stopped. After that I reckoned I wouldn't have long to wait.

So I went into the bathroom and soaked my head in cold water. When I came back and sat guard again I'd lost the desire to sleep.

Nothing happened after that for maybe a couple or three minutes. It was crowding half after eleven when I heard the distant wail of a siren. As it came rapidly nearer I sat watching the hallway door. The way it added up one thing had nothing to do with another.

I was wrong. The cruiser took only

another few seconds to clear the inter-section and come howling down my home street.

It wailed to a stop right outside the apartment block. Car doors slammed . . . feet slapped across the sidewalk . . . at least two pairs of feet clattered up the stairs.

I put the .38 out of sight but not out of reach. By the time I'd got up and shifted the chair back where it belonged the hurrying feet were almost at my door.

Even then I couldn't be sure. But I was soon left in no doubt.

A set of hard knuckles banged half a dozen times. When they stopped, I said, "Who is that?"

Somebody with gravel in his throat said, "Police. Open up." His voice matched the knuckles.

With my hand not far from the butt of the Smith and Wesson I turned the key and pulled the door open as far as my right foot would let it. That was enough to give me a good view of two hard-faced crewmen. The one nearest me was carrying a police positive. His face looked like it had been hacked out of a lump of rock.

It was his sidekick who did the talking. He had black eyebrows, dark stubble on his jowls and an Irish accent.

He said, "If you take your foot away we'll come in. And I hope you won't start asking what we'll do if you don't."

They seemed kosher but that didn't prove a darn thing. I said, "This is my place and the rent's paid up to the end of the month. Before you come in here I want to see some proof of identity."

Both of them studied me like I had no clothes on. Then the mick said, "You got it wrong way round. We're here to find out who you are. Don't make a fuss or you'll disturb the neighbours."

I said, "That would suit me fine. They'll tell you my name's Bowman and I live in this apartment and — "

" — and the rent's paid up to the end of the month." His face creased in a smile that didn't show his teeth. "In case you don't know what day it is that only takes you to Wednesday night. Can you prove

123

you're Bowman?"

"Soon as you prove you're entitled to wear that uniform."

He felt in his pocket and brought out a warrant card. He said, "Take a look at this . . . but don't let your hand stray anywhere near that gun you've got stuck in your pants."

The warrant card was genuine. When I'd given it back to him I opened the door wide and both of them came in.

Then it was my turn. I showed the mick my operator's licence and some letters addressed to me and my permit for the Smith and Wesson. After he'd examined them all the atmosphere mellowed somewhat.

In a relaxed voice, he asked, "Mind if I look around?"

I said, "Help yourself . . . providing you answer a couple of questions when you're satisfied there's nobody here but us three."

"Sure thing. Why not?"

His sidekick put away the police positive but his eyes never left my face. He kept me company while the mick carried out a brief search of bathroom and bedroom.

It took less than a minute. He looked under my bed, glanced in the clothes closet and finally made a quick survey of the living-room.

If he'd raised his sights above eye-level he'd have spotted the hole in the plaster that the .45 slug had made but he didn't. Neither did he see the splintered hole in the window. I was glad of that. I didn't want to get involved in explanations that would explain nothing.

When he was all through, he said, "Guess we were given a bum steer." He sounded disappointed and he looked like he thought it was my fault.

I said, "That's my first question. What did you expect to find?"

"You — out for the long count. We got a buzz you'd been anticipating trouble and you didn't answer the phone although you should've been here."

"Who phoned me?"

"A guy called Ed Killick. He's a special investigator working for the DA. Know him?"

"Yes, I know him all right."

"Well, he says he dialled your number ten-fifteen minutes ago and got no reply."

"Too bad," I said. "I didn't hear the bell."

With his black eyebrows pulled down in a bushy straight line, the mick glanced from me to the phone to his sidekick and back to me again. He asked, "How come?"

"I was in the shower. Didn't think anyone was likely to call me at half after eleven or I'd have left the bedroom door open. If Killick had waited five minutes and tried again there wouldn't have been all this excitement."

"What made him think you might be in some kind of trouble?"

"My racket breeds trouble," I said. "When you spend your life poking into other people's business you make enemies."

"Why would Mr Killick pick on tonight instead of any other night?"

In the uneasy depths of my mind, Ed Killick was saying " . . . *Plenty of people in this town who won't be keen to*

126

have a guy like you turning over various damp rocks to see what crawls out. And they have their own way of dealing with snoopers."

I said, "He stopped by for a chat tonight and we talked about some hard-boiled characters who play rough. He knew I was going to hit the hay after he left and so I guess he jumped to hasty conclusions when I didn't answer the phone."

"Could be — " the mick wasn't satisfied but there was very little he could do about it — "yeh, could be."

"Sorry to have got you in a lather," I said.

"Think nothing of it. All part of the job." He nodded to the one with the face chipped out of granite. "Let's go."

Then he looked at me and added, "You might give Mr Killick a ring and tell him you're still alive."

"I'll do that," I said. "Thanks for the service."

"Any time." He grinned at me again like he had no teeth. "We don't treat a private eye any different from good-class

127

citizens. 'Night . . . "

They went out and pulled the door shut and two pairs of feet clumped their way out of step to the top of the stairs. I heard them go on down . . . car doors banged . . . somebody gunned the motor in a fast take-off.

A while after they'd gone I drew the living-room drapes and fixed myself a short drink. As I checked Ed Killick's number in the book the phone rang.

I'd have laid dollars to doughnuts it was Killick. When I picked up the receiver I reckoned this was my night for being wrong all along the line.

Henderson said, "I knew it couldn't be true. Things like that just don't happen."

"What things?"

"They told me you'd be retiring permanently to your country estate. I was getting all ready to attend my second funeral in one week . . . and you go and disappoint me. If you had any consideration — "

"Who told you?"

"Killick. Who else? He tried to contact

128

you and got no reply. So he gave me a buzz. I asked the local precinct to send a squad car. They've just called in to say you don't know what all the fuss is about. Now let's hear why you didn't answer the phone when Killick rang."

I said, "I explained that to the crew who were here. I was in the shower and — "

" — and you didn't hear the phone bell ringing." Henderson's voice came nearer and louder. "Maybe they believed you, maybe not. I don't. If that's your story, don't try sticking to it. I want the real reason why Killick got no reply. So — give."

As I saw it, sooner or later he'd get to know the truth. I said, "I'll give it to you straight but it'll have to be off the record."

"What makes you think you can lay down your own conditions?"

"It's either that or no dice."

Either he needed time to think it over or he wanted me to think he needed time. He took long enough before he said, "All

129

right. Unless circumstances change, it's off the record."

I said, "Then hear this. Around eleven o'clock tonight my circumstances darn near changed for keeps. Somebody took a shot at me through my living-room window . . . and I've got a .45 slug to prove it."

He took some more time out. At last, he said, "You sound healthy enough. Evidently the shot missed."

"If it hadn't — and by a damn' narrow margin — I'd have had a very evident hole in the middle of my face."

"Did you catch sight of the party who took a crack at you?"

"No, I was too busy diving to the floor. After a while I crawled into the bedroom and collected my gun . . . "

Henderson listened, grunted once or twice to let me know he was still listening and waited until he'd heard it all. Then he asked, "Would you say the shot came from the street or from some place opposite?"

"Judging by the angle it must've been fired by somebody on the opposite sidewalk. I heard footsteps crossing to my side and a car came along not more than a couple of minutes later . . . but your guess is as good as mine whether the two things were connected."

"You've still got the slug you dug out of the wall?"

"Sure. You want it?"

"Yes. I'd like Ballistics to check it with the one that put paid to Frank Siccola."

"Two gets you five it came from the same gun," I said.

"You must be the last of the big-time gamblers. I'll offer you ten-to-one it was the same .45 automatic. But I still want confirmation that would stand up in a court of law."

"Assuming you ever get your hands on the gun."

"Why not? The chances are better now than they were before."

"How?"

"Somebody thinks you might get too close for comfort. There can't be any other reason for what happened tonight."

"That's another assumption," I said.

"Unless you believe in wild coincidence,

it must be more than just an assumption when the same calibre of gun was used."

"The same calibre but not necessarily the same gun. A .45 automatic isn't all that unusual."

Henderson said, "You're too fond of arguing both ways at once. You know and I know it was the same gun. Somebody found out you'd been hired by Miss Russell to hunt for Frankie's killer. Somebody doesn't like the idea. So somebody thought you should be stopped before you got started. Isn't that how it adds up?"

"Well, it seems logical."

"Right. But there's one detail that leaves me out in the cold. You must've learned something about Frank Siccola's death that I don't know . . . and you've learned it since we attended his funeral this morning. Now what could that be?"

"Nothing relevant to the identity of his killer," I said.

"No?"

"Positively no. If I knew who gunned Siccola do you think I'd keep it to myself?"

"I hope not. But convincing me won't convince the party who took a shot at you through the window. Next time might be the last time."

"There won't be a next time," I said. "I don't intend to stand in front of any windows with the light at my back."

The phone made no comment for all of ten seconds. Then Henderson asked, "Why didn't you tell the crew of the prowl car?"

"Because I don't want any fuss that won't produce any results."

"How do you know?"

"Experience. They'd have asked me a lot of questions to which I didn't know the answers . . . and I've already had a long, busy day."

"You're not the only one."

"Glad to hear it. Seeing you feel like I feel you won't mind if I hang up . . . will you?"

"No, I won't mind at all. Just one thing more."

"Such as . . . ?"

"The prowl car reported that you were carrying a gun."

133

"That's right. I was and I am."

"You're wise," Henderson said. "If I were you I'd keep it handy at all times. Sleep tight . . ."

* * *

I finished my nightcap and got into pyjamas. My bedside clock told me I'd already lost best part of half an hour's sleep.

As I sat down on the edge of the bed and kicked off my slippers I remembered Ed Killick. It hardly seemed necessary to call him. Somebody would've told him by now that all the excitement had been a false alarm — Henderson or somebody. They were bound to have told him.

And yet . . . He'd put himself out for me. If I'd been in trouble it could've made all the difference between living and dying. The least I could do to show my appreciation . . .

About then the phone rang. It went through me like an electric shock. When I'd quit twitching I began to get mad.

Whatever Henderson wanted it would've

134

kept until morning. Another few hours could scarcely be all that important. Apart from which I was in no mood for his brand of humour. I'd had just about as much ribbing as I could take.

It wasn't Henderson. It was Ed Killick.

He said, "I've just heard from your pal in Homicide that you nearly got what Siccola got."

"Henderson's no pal of mine," I said. "But his information's correct. I've been wondering if it was too late to ring you and say thanks for calling out the marines."

"Don't mention it. Glad they weren't needed. When I got no reply from your number I wasn't sure what was the best thing to do. Eventually I decided there'd be no harm in passing the buck to Henderson."

"You did right. Incidentally, now all the song and dance is over, what did you want to talk about when you tried to call me?"

"Oh, nothing really urgent." He sounded amused. "On my way home after I left your place I stopped by at the office and found a report from the operator who's been keeping tabs on Mrs Connie Siccola. Seems she's had some interesting visitors this evening."

"Including me," I said.

"But yes. You arrived at eight o'clock and left at eight-thirty . . . give or take. Check?"

"Near enough. I didn't spot your stake-out. He must be good."

"He's trained to be good."

In the same tone, Killick added, "I don't know what went on between you and that blonde twist . . . but Theo Prager was her next visitor and he drove up like he was in one helluva hurry. Before I shut up shop for the night I thought I'd better tell you — just in case. Prager is real mean."

Connie's small voice was talking inside my head. " . . . *You're different from all the other guys . . . Kiss me goodbye like you were my friend.*" Once again the sweet taste of her lips was on my mouth. Once again I could see that look of innocence in her blue, blue eyes.

It was always the same. Connie could never be anything to me. Connie was just a dumb, beautiful tramp.

I said, "Nothing went on between me and Siccola's widow — nothing that the All-American Women's Purity League couldn't have witnessed. I'd have thought that would be in your stake-out's report."

Ed Killick was still amused. It showed in his voice when he said, "Our stake-out isn't eighteen feet tall."

"What's that supposed to mean?"

"He can't peek through bedroom windows."

Maybe I'd have expected that sort of crack from Henderson but coming from Killick it riled me. I said, "Whatever ideas you have about her, if you think I'd go to her husband's funeral in the morning and then go to bed with her the same night you must have a lousy opinion of me."

He said, "Keep your shirt on. You haven't seen Connie's file — I have. It makes Fanny Hill read like a report on a church social. With her looks she's a man-eater."

"Well, she'd find me a tough morsel," I said. "For your information we spent half an hour discussing Frankie Siccola and the life she had with him. That was all."

"OK. OK. I believe you. But you don't know what she told Theo Prager or what Prager suspected had happened. I have an idea he's always fancied moving into Frankie's place. And now Frankie's out of the way — "

"You're saying it was Prager who took a shot at me."

"No . . . but it's worth thinking about. I know his kind. That's why I tried to call you when I learned he'd visited the house on Riverside Drive not long after you left . . . "

The more I thought about Killick's theory, the more it made sense. If Prager had a yen for Connie . . . and if Prager had discovered that Frankie was sitting on half a million dollars' worth of cut gems . . . and Frankie was about to skip the country . . .

It all added up. Prager had a double motive for disposing of Siccola. By the same reasoning he had a good motive plus for getting me out of his hair.

I said, "Didn't you tell me you've been keeping a tail on Prager ever since the night Frankie was shot to death?"

"We were. But not after the funeral. Haven't got enough man-power."

"So he might've been anywhere around eleven o'clock tonight?"

"That's right," Killick said. "And anywhere includes the street outside your apartment."

"How long do you intend to keep tabs on Miss Russell and Connie Siccola?"

"Another twelve hours. The DA doesn't think it's going to serve any purpose after that."

"Hasn't seemed to have done much good up to now," I said.

"Well — " Ed Killick sounded ruffled — "you can't win 'em all. We'll see if you can do any better."

"Must be past your bedtime," I said. "You're getting touchy. I didn't mean to rub you the wrong way."

"No offence taken." He yawned a couple of times and cleared his throat.

"I'm dog-tired — that's all. I could sleep standing up."

"Then let's call it a day. Thanks again for what you did. I appreciate it."

"You'd do the same for me," Killick said. "Instead of thanks I'll still settle for a piece of co-operation. 'Night . . . "

* * *

Long after I should've been asleep I lay awake, my mind filled with a confusion of thoughts like irregular steps leading me up to a pinnacle where I'd find the answer to all my questions. I could see that small group around the grave of Frankie Siccola . . . spadeful after spadeful of clay beating a tattoo on his coffin . . . the parson's whining voice, his boneless face peaky with cold.

Behind them all there was the faceless one who'd been outside in the street with a .45 automatic. As I lay watching the thin crescent of moon in its last quarter I had a morbid picture of what might have happened if the shot had been two-three inches to the left.

Instead of lying in a warm comfortable bed I'd have been stiffening in a drawer down at the city morgue. An Irish auto-cop and his team-mate would be sweating out their report on what they'd found when they entered my flatlet in response to a radio call.

I wouldn't know and I wouldn't care. Nothing would matter any more — neither Connie who trusted me nor Diane whom I didn't trust. People would say I'd been asking for trouble all my life and finally it had caught up with me.

. . . Another hole in the ground . . . another headstone with its routine inscription: *Deeply mourned . . . RIP . . .*

The arc of the moon hung in a frosty nimbus just outside my window, its light slicing my room in two with a silver knife. In the greater darkness beyond the moonlight my imagination could see things which exist only in that hour when the old day is dying and the new day has yet to be born.

Henderson . . . and Ed Killick . . . and a moron called Prager. It could have been

Prager who had watched and waited in the street with a .45 automatic.

On the threshold of sleep I wondered if Killick would've changed his mind if I'd told him what Diane Russell had told me about the man who'd been betrayed by Frankie Siccola. Then I wondered why the DA's operators hadn't seen anything of Jeff Connolly. They'd know him if they saw him . . . they were bound to know him. He was being hunted by every law-enforcement officer from coast to coast.

The question was how long he could move around and yet remain out of sight. It wasn't the only question.

My life was worth more than a five thousand dollar cut of the reward. To earn the money I had to stay alive. It would be a whole lot easier to stay alive if I took Ed Killick's advice and left town for a while . . . and the hell with Shoemaker Gem Corporation's parcel of diamonds . . .

Guess I must've drifted over the threshold about there. It was the phone bell that prodded me awake.

How long I'd been asleep I didn't know but the crescent of moon was still in the same place so it couldn't have been very long. Yet my wits were wrapped in cotton-wool as though I'd slept for a hundred nights. As I tumbled out of bed I hardly knew where I was.

Twice I bumped into something in the darkness beyond the shaft of moonlight. Twice I cursed the damn' bell that rang and stopped . . . and rang and rang and rang . . .

Then at last I got hold of the receiver. When I'd managed to find my voice, I said, "Yes? Who is that?"

All I got in reply was nothing. I knew my phone was connected to some other phone because I could hear the empty quiet humming of an open wire. So I wasn't talking to myself. What griped me was that I might as well.

After I'd asked the same question again and nobody answered, I said, "Look. You got a wrong number. I'm no old maid to be scared by the sound of heavy breathing. And four-letter words don't shock me, either. I could teach you a few that would make your hair — "

That was when I heard it. Faint at first but getting nearer and louder every moment I could hear the ticking of a clock.

Just a clock . . . an ordinary clock. It sounded like my alarm back in the bedroom . . . only louder and nearer. Now it seemed to be inside my head.

Why the ticking of a clock should've given me goose-pimples is something I've never been able to understand. But it did. And why I didn't just hang up is something else I couldn't explain.

Anyway, the whole thing didn't last more than fifteen or twenty seconds. Just when my head felt like it was going to burst wide open the damn' ticking stopped . . . like the beating of a man's heart at the moment of death.

And that was all. Next moment the wire went dead and I was left shivering in the darkness of my living-room like a scared kid alone in an empty house with spectres of his own creation.

When I got back into bed I was still shivering. I couldn't put a name to the

party who'd been at the other end of
the wire but I knew who it must be.
And the thought of that faceless one
kept me company until at last I fell
asleep.

6

TUESDAY, October 30, was another cold day. It had snowed a little during the night — just enough snow to dust sidewalks and pavement with a fine layer of sugar icing that was already criss-crossed with tyre tracks and jumbled footprints.

As I shaved, showered and got my clothes on I found myself thinking of days long ago when snow had been fun: toboggan rides down a long winding slope not far from home . . . a sing-song with college friends ringed round a spluttering camp fire that grew brighter as dusk turned to darkness . . . that girl who had snuggled close to me, her eyes shining in the light of the flames.

I couldn't remember her face or her name or how we had met. Too much had happened in the years between. Yet I could still smell the drifting smoke, the aromatic tang of burning pine cones.

Elusive memories of once-upon-a-time were hard to shake off. They seemed to belong to another man's life but they still clung to me while I fixed myself a cup of coffee. I even had a damnfool notion that it would be nice to meet that girl again.

A voice in my head told me she probably had a flock of kids by now. She wouldn't know me any more than I'd know her. The worst thing of all would be if we did. It never paid to go back. Only those who were immature tried to recapture the past.

Maybe I was in there somewhere. Maybe my trouble was that I hadn't grown up.

The nagging voice asked me if I'd only just realized it. I washed him down the sink along with the dregs of my coffee.

Eight-thirty I got to the office. No one had followed me across town, no one was waiting for me when I unlocked the door. It looked like someone had taken too much for granted.

The central heating was on but it

hadn't had time to build up. My dog-kennel registered a temperature of not much more than 55°F. I kept my topcoat on while I used the phone.

A man in Homicide wasn't sure if Captain Henderson had arrived yet. " . . . Mind holding the wire while I go see . . . or will somebody else do?"

When I told him I'd hold he went away and I was left to my day-dreams of an evening long ago and the pictures I'd seen in the glowing heart of a camp fire in the snow. It helped to kill time while I waited.

Then Henderson asked, "What do you want?" He sounded like the weather had got into his bones.

"The answer to one simple question," I said.

"Why don't you find your own answers? That's what you're being paid for, isn't it?"

"Not this one. It's about Jeff Connolly's wife . . . assuming he's married, of course."

"His marriage is fact, not assumption. Her name's Pamela and they're legally wed. Now if that's all . . . "

I said, "You sound like you fell out of bed this morning. I haven't got to my question yet."

"All right, let's hear it. And don't cut a short story long. I've got a busy day ahead of me."

"Me, too. So you can make it brief. Have you spoken with Pamela Connolly since you put out an all-stations for her husband?"

Henderson cleared his throat. He said, "No, I haven't. That brief enough for you?"

"It would be . . . except that it isn't an answer. Why haven't you?"

"Because she'd cleared out when we went calling on her."

"After Tew was found dead?"

"Not right then. At that time we had no reason to suspect that Connolly and Tew were involved in the Shoemaker Gem Corporation job. It wasn't until the following day that we got the tip-off."

"Who squealed?"

"If I knew I wouldn't tell you," Henderson said.

"All right, keep your shirt on. How did your anonymous informant make contact?"

"By phone. The call was put through to me. To save you asking, it was a man's voice — any man's voice. When he'd said what he had to say he hung up. I never got a chance to trace the call or even put it on tape."

"Did he give you Jeff Connolly's address?"

"Oh, sure. By the time we got there our chickens had flown the coop."

"Learn anything of interest from the neighbours?"

"Not much. Nobody had seen Connolly around for quite some time. His wife had been living in the apartment — seemingly all by herself — right up to the previous day."

"So she ducked out just before you got the tip-off?"

"Apparently. And don't tell me it's too much of a coincidence — I know. Instead you might explain your preoccupation with Pamela Connolly."

"Find the wife and she may lead you

to the husband," I said.

"Meaning you still think he could've been implicated in the shooting of Frankie Siccola?"

"What I think is based on what I'm told. And he's on Diane Russell's list of suspects."

Henderson said, "More important is that you're on her payroll. Are you just dancing to Miss Russell's tune or do you really believe it was Connolly?"

"The answer to that is twice no," I said. "Until I've had a chat with Connolly's wife it's all guesswork."

"Including the motive?"

"You could say that."

In a changed voice, Henderson asked, "Why can't you say it? Or are you holding out on me?"

I said, "Look. Homicide have been working on this case since last Wednesday night. You've also had a file on Frankie Siccola that goes back years. You know what he was and how he operated. If you can't think of a motive it's just too bad."

After a long pause for thought, Henderson

said, "The old double-X . . . I suppose it's possible, more than possible. The question is where Pamela Connolly is hiding out."

"And the answer might be a matter of urgency."

"Yeh. There's always the risk her husband may find her before we do."

"The odds are in your favour," I said.

"Guess so. But her chances would be a lot better if we had Connolly behind bars."

In the same tone, Henderson added, "So would yours . . . if the events of last night are anything to go on. Wonder why he thinks he has to get rid of you?"

I said, "That's something else again . . . "

★ ★ ★

The phone book didn't list anyone called Pamela Connolly at Lakeland Towers. I hadn't expected it would. Whatever name she was living under made no difference so long as she still lived at apartment 412.

All the same there was no sense in

traipsing uptown to Eighty-Fifth Street just to find she wasn't home. So I checked the book again.

Sullivans were a dime a dozen. No Pamela, no initials P at Lakeland Towers.

When I'd thought about it I asked myself why she might not have adopted Frankie's initial as well as the phoney name he'd used to sign the register at Duffie's Hotel. Always a chance that the apartment had been taken under a different name altogether . . . but Sullivan was as good as any.

My guess was that Frankie wouldn't have wanted to chop and change. Too many fake names might be confusing. So the odds were he'd chosen Sullivan when he checked in at Duffie's place because he'd already been using it . . .

I'd guessed right. There was an F. Sullivan at apartment 412. No mention whether it was a he or a she but that hardly mattered. Connie had trailed Siccola to Lakeland Towers. Connie had satisfied herself he was lovenesting in 412.

A minor puzzle was how she'd known the other woman was called Pamela.

Could be she'd assumed he wasn't drawing cheques in favour of one playmate and keeping another at Lakeland Towers. I reckoned it was logical.

The phone went on ringing for a long time. I began to get the idea that Jeff Connolly's wife had done another fade-out. Maybe she'd gone off with her husband. Maybe Connie was all wrong about Pamela's relationship with Frankie. Or maybe Diane Russell was dealing from the bottom of the deck.

It had happened to me before. How she could hope to make it pay off was another matter . . . if she'd been lying. If . . .

Then the phone asked, "Yes? Who is that?"

Nothing special about her voice. She didn't sound either cultured or common . . . or sexy, for that matter. A woman straddling thirty was my guess — a woman who seemed kind of nervous.

I said, "This is Same-Day Cleaning Service. Am I speaking to Mrs Telford?"

"No . . . no, you got a wrong number." Judging by her tone she didn't know whether to be scared or relieved. "There's no one of that name here."

"My apologies," I said. "I'm sorry you've — "

There I quit talking to myself. She'd hung up on me.

* * *

A quarter after nine the cab dropped me on the corner of Eighty-Fifth and Lexington. I walked the rest of the way to Lakeland Towers.

It looked even more expensive by day. There were some quality folks in the lobby but none I'd ever seen before. I wasn't surprised. I didn't mix much with the kind of people who lived in that kind of place.

A woman who was over-weight, over-dressed and over fifty shared the elevator with me as far as the third floor. I rode on up to the fourth.

It was as quiet up there as it had been last night. I could almost hear my own footsteps in the deep-pile carpet when I followed the arrow pointing left: *Nos. 410 – 418*

155

Before I reached No. 412 I heard the elevator go back down. It didn't interest me one tiny bit. I was totally concerned with the fact that Mrs Connolly's apartment door was open — not much but enough to let me see into the little entrance hall.

I touched the white bell-push and it buzzed discreetly. At the same time the pressure of my finger eased the door another few inches. Now I could see across the hall and into a room where the door had been left wide open.

It was a bedroom with cream-and-gold furniture and cream-and-gold decor. A pair of fluffy mules stood under the foot of a big double bed. Not far away lay what looked like a pair of nylons and a wrap that had been dropped carelessly on the floor. From where I stood the angle was too narrow to let me see anything else.

A second touch on the buzzer got me no more answer than the first. I took a short step into the hall and called out "Anyone home?"

There wasn't a sound. It was so quiet

I could hear the ticking of a clock in the bedroom.

That tick-tick-tick-tick reminded me of the phone call that had got me out of bed. Crazy or not, I felt my skin creep again. The same atmosphere of menace was all around me once more.

Another step widened the angle. Another step revealed what I hadn't been able to see before. And what I saw gave me a real dose of goose-pimples.

Maybe I should've minded my own business. If I were caught trespassing it would mean trouble. An open door didn't give me any right to walk into apartment 412 . . .

At times like that my legs seem to go places I don't want them to go. Next thing I knew I'd taken a third step.

And next thing I knew I didn't know anything. That final step brought me beyond the leading edge of the door.

I heard nothing, saw nothing, felt nothing. My front foot never touched the floor . . . because the floor had disappeared . . . and I'd stepped over the brink of a bottomless pit.

★ ★ ★

Waking was hell. I wanted to stop down there and forget all the things that were prodding me with red-hot spikes to get up and think and live again. For my part I wished I was dead.

It lasted a long time . . . or it seemed that way. I reckoned I must've been suspended between darkness and light for a thousand years before at last I realized what had happened and why my skull split in fragments with every beat of the big vein in my neck.

I hadn't thought there might be someone hidden behind the door. I'd got what I'd asked for. I'd walked in where I wasn't wanted.

Like part of a dream I remembered something I'd seen just before I'd taken that last step. Something in the bedroom . . . something I could've imagined . . . something that explained why I'd been slugged.

With my eyes screwed tight I lay and sweated while wave after wave of pain swept through my head. Dimly I

158

wondered how it came that I was still alive. The opportunity had been there to get rid of me for keeps. Yet I was still alive . . .

The pain ebbed and flowed. It was becoming less . . . just a little. Now I could locate where I'd been hit. Now I began to think I hadn't been meant to die.

Gradually awareness of my surroundings returned. I was lying on a bed — not in bed but on top of a silky eiderdown. I could feel the cool smoothness of it on my skin. It caressed shoulders and back and legs . . . even my feet.

That was when I discovered I was stark naked. That was when I forced my eyes open.

The only light in the room came from a bedside lamp — just a small lamp in the shape of a figurine with a gold-tasselled shade. It was enough light to show me I was in the bedroom of apartment 412 at Lakeland Towers.

My eyes hurt badly. I shut them again and sweated some more while I tried to make sense where none existed.

Somebody had used a sap on me: that I could understand. Somebody had lugged me into the bedroom and stripped my clothes off: that I couldn't understand. It served no purpose . . .

Once again a piece of that half-forgotten dream came back to me. If it weren't a dream it made sense in a crazy sort of way. If it weren't a dream . . .

I put a hand over my eyes and opened them just enough to let the light seep in. They didn't hurt so much now. It was the burning pain in my head that troubled me. Whenever I tried to move it seared through me like a branding iron.

So I lay still and collected my thoughts into some kind of pattern. There was always a reason for everything . . . if only I could find it.

Time went by while I drifted to and fro on the borders of reality. After a while I discovered something new. My clothes had gone but I still had my wrist-watch.

I turned my hand over and brought the watch close to my eyes. When the figures on the dial quit swimming around they said the time was twenty-five minutes off ten.

That meant . . . My mind wandered off and I had to drag it back again. Slowly and laboriously I did a simple calculation.

I'd paid off the cab at nine-fifteen. When I got to Lakeland Towers it was close on half after nine . . . give or take a couple of minutes. Allow that couple of minutes for the ride in the elevator up to the fourth floor and the time I'd loitered outside apartment 412 . . .

Two minutes was an ample allowance. And the answer it gave was nine-thirty.

All that left me was five minutes to account for. However long it had seemed I'd been out cold for no more than five minutes.

The pain in my head was beginning to subside. If I breathed little shallow breaths I could hold on to my thoughts and make co-ordinated movements.

One thing I knew without thinking. I had to find my clothes. That came before all else.

With infinite caution I rolled over on

to my right side. The room pitched and dipped like an old coaster breasting the tide and sudden nausea made me want to throw up. I had to hold on until my stomach went back down where it belonged. Then I manoeuvred myself into a sitting position.

Now I could see through the open bedroom door and across the little hall. The outer door was shut. There was no one in the hall, no sign of the party who'd stepped out as I stepped in and beat me over the head.

My clothes lay in an untidy heap between the foot of the bed and the doorway. Not far from them were the nylons and the wrap I'd seen while I was standing outside the apartment. They belonged to what I knew must be the figment of that dream.

When I turned my head a little bit at a time I saw the drapes were drawn. That accounted for the bedside lamp. At half after nine on a fairly bright morning there would've been enough light without needing to switch on the lamp.

Random thoughts played leap-frog in my mind. Perhaps she'd been getting dressed . . . and she hadn't wanted anyone to play Peeping Tom . . . because some of the other apartments overlooked hers . . . and my phone call had got her out of bed . . . and she'd thrown some clothes on in a hurry.

Perhaps . . . perhaps . . . It didn't explain how she'd known I was going to visit with her and why she'd waited behind the door and also why it had been necessary to leave me in the raw.

Asking myself questions to which there were no answers only made my head throb all the more. When I felt the hot lump just below my crown I reckoned it could've been worse. The lining of my hat must have cushioned part of the blow. If it hadn't, the chances were I'd have been dead.

Thoughts and movements were all in slow motion. I never got round to wondering where she'd gone. I only wanted to put some clothes on and bathe my throbbing head and then get the hell out of this nuthouse.

163

Very carefully I lowered myself over the edge of the bed until my bare feet rested on the carpet. When I got that far I had to hang on while the room sunfished, my eyes tight shut, my stomach protesting violently. Right then I felt real sorry for myself.

What didn't help was the old nagging voice telling me it was all my own fault. How it was my fault I neither knew nor cared. All I wanted was to go some place and find a nice quiet corner where I could lie down and die.

The churning sensation lasted for what seemed a long time. The whole of that time I stood there in my birthday suit clinging to the bed and hating Pamela Connolly for what she'd done to me.

It wasn't necessary to understand why she'd stripped me down to my wrist-watch. Maybe she'd wanted to make sure I couldn't follow her.

Maybe this, maybe that. It didn't matter. How she'd managed to heave me on to the bed didn't matter, either.

The nausea grew less and the pain in

my head settled down to the beating of a tom-tom. I reckoned I could risk opening my eyes.

That sure was a mistake. Soon as I was able to focus I realized why I'd been left in a state of nature.

There were two of us in the cream-and-gold bedroom. I'd never met the other one before and I had no itch to meet her again.

She was lying stark naked on the bed within an arm's length of where I'd been lying — a dainty doll with jet-black hair, grey eyes and nicely-moulded features. The rest of her — firm breasts, trim waist, long slim legs — would've been nice, too, in other circumstances.

Her lips were parted in what might have been a smile if there'd been anything to smile at. Me, I couldn't see the joke in a couple of strangers playing Adam and Eve.

It was her eyes that told me she didn't think it was all that funny, either. They stared up into mine with the kind of look that said there was no one home.

At first glance she looked like she'd fallen asleep with her eyes open. I didn't need a second glance to know she wouldn't wake up this side of Judgment Day.

7

HASTE and recurring dizziness made me clumsy. With hands that were all thumbs I began to get dressed.

Stooping to fasten my shoes was bad. I fell over twice, picked myself up and struggled on. All the time I kept imagining I could hear the wail of a siren.

By then I was respectable from the waist down. By then I had a feeling of embarrassment at the idea that she was lying there without a stitch, her dead grey eyes watching me as though from a long way off.

The whole set-up was wrong. Even if it made no difference to her it mattered a lot to me. I couldn't bear the thought that I was taking part in an obscene performance.

That's how it would look if someone walked in while I was putting my shirt on. If someone walked in . . . if someone walked in . . .

I covered her with the lower half of the eiderdown and kept it from slipping off with the pair of mules from under the bed. Her feet stuck out but that couldn't be helped. The main thing was that she'd no longer be able to watch me.

In another minute or two I was fully dressed except for my hat. I couldn't put it on because the lump on my head hurt like the devil . . . yet I had to wear it so I wouldn't be identified later if someone saw me leaving the apartment. Somehow or other I had to wear it.

So I looked around until I located the bathroom. Then I immersed my head in a basin of ice-cold water.

It helped. After the first ecstatic shock it brought a greater relief than I'd hoped for. As I towelled my hair I could think straight again.

Now everything formed a pattern. Someone had been with Pamela Connolly when I called her on the phone. Someone must've guessed that the call wasn't a wrong number. Someone also guessed she'd be having another visitor very soon.

And Pamela couldn't be allowed to talk. If nothing else she'd have been able to betray the identity of that someone. But if she died it would kill two birds with one stone . . . if her visitor walked into the trap like a fool — like me.

She'd been laid on the floor beside the bed so I'd catch sight of her and go rushing in and get put to sleep. When both of us were dumped side by side on the bed the frame was complete.

I was supposed to remain unconscious long enough for the law to arrive. Then it wouldn've been a case of my story against all the facts — my story supported by a lump on my head. I didn't reckon that would carry much weight.

More and more clearly I remembered the fragment of a dream that had lingered in my mind when I came back to the here and now. It had been the glimpse of a woman's arm with outspread hand that I'd seen half-concealed by the bed.

If I hadn't recovered when I did I'd have wakened from a dream into a nightmare. They'd have found us together on the bed like something painted by Rubens — something I wouldn't have had a cat-in-hell's chance of explaining away.

This woman and I had shared the same bed, naked as the day we were born. On or in the bed made no difference. The law would say that we were like that because she'd been the victim of assault. The law would say a lot of things I couldn't refute.

Now I had to get out of apartment 412 — but fast. My watch said the time was nearly twenty minutes off ten. They'd be arriving soon . . . all too soon. I knew that same as I knew I'd been meant to be the patsy.

Better to frame me for the death of Pamela Connolly than to put a .45 slug in my head . . . like Frankie Siccola. Either way somebody would get me out of his hair. And this way there'd be fewer questions asked.

Before I left I had to have the answer to one more question. It would take only a matter of seconds and I had to know . . . even if time was running out for me.

Down below on Eighty-Fifth Street the traffic rolled by just like it always did. No sirens, no excitement. In the hallway outside 412 everything was quiet as well.

Maybe I was poco loco from that bang on the head. Now I know I should've gone while the going was good. Right then I convinced myself that another few seconds couldn't make much difference.

One thing for sure was that Pamela didn't mind. When I lifted a corner of the eiderdown she was still looking up at me with the same vacant expression in her eyes. That synthetic smile hadn't changed, either.

I put a hand under one shoulder and turned her over face-down. She felt warm to the touch — as warm as though still alive. But her skin was lax as the skin of a dead chicken.

It took only one quick glance to confirm that there weren't any marks of violence on her back. From head to waist I could see no bruises, no wounds, no blood. If she'd been in bed and wearing a nightgown I'd have thought death had come in her sleep.

So I had my answer. But it wasn't an answer.

She didn't look like she'd been poisoned. The pupils of her eyes seemed normal. When I sniffed at her open mouth I couldn't detect the odour of anything unusual . . . not even alcohol. It would've been unusual for a woman to smell of liquor around nine o'clock of a morning.

There was no apparent cause of death but she was all the same dead. As I covered her again with the eiderdown I told myself it was for the experts to decide how and why she'd died when they performed an autopsy.

Meanwhile trouble would be coming my way any minute now. Only one explanation fitted this whole set-up.

With a handkerchief wrapped round my fingers I went into the little hall and pulled the bedroom door shut nice and quietly. Three-four steps brought me to the outer door.

All the time I was listening for the

distant howl of a siren. It had to be that way . . . unless they'd cut the siren so as to give me a surprise. That meant they might be riding up in the elevator. It also meant I'd walk out as they were about to walk in.

Outside in the hallway I thought I heard muted footsteps. They seemed to be going farther away but I couldn't be sure. So I leaned against the door and held my breath and listened.

The footsteps had gone. In their place I could faintly hear a mosaic of far-off sounds: a phone bell that rang momentarily . . . the hum of a vacuum cleaner . . . a scarcely audible thread of music.

On the other side of the door all was quiet. I knew this might be my last chance. More than ten minutes had gone by since I'd been put to sleep — long enough for someone to have called the police and for a prowl car to arrive.

That must've been the whole idea. Stripping me down to the buff served no other purpose. I was meant to be caught with no hope of escape . . . no hope . . . no hope . . .

The words repeated themselves over and over again in my mind as I heard footsteps padding along the hallway from the direction of the elevator. When they were only a few paces away I drew back and stood very still.

The muffled thump-thump-thump-thump of solid footsteps came level with apartment 412. Then they halted.

For all of twenty seconds I heard laboured breathing, the brush of clothing against the door. A voice grumbled huskily " . . . O dear, o dear, o dear. Time you took some weight off. The doctor says you're carrying twenty pounds of extra fat and it don't do you no good, that's for sure . . . "

It was a woman's voice. I'd have said her ancestors had spent their days picking cotton.

She quit talking to herself and panted some more. I could only stand there and let the nagging voice in my head tell me I'd thrown away my big chance by loitering a quarter of a minute too long.

There was nowhere I could hide,

nothing I could do. My only hope was that she'd go away if she got no answer . . . if she didn't think it was queer when no one answered . . . if she didn't kick up a fuss . . .

Must've been just about then that the buzzer drilled a hole clean through the tender spot in my head. It nearly knocked me over. And while my heart was playing hop-scotch that damn' buzzer sounded off again.

This time it didn't give me palpitations. Before she tried a third time I'd turned my coat collar up and pulled the brim of my hat down low. If black mama got the idea something was very wrong and whistled up reinforcements, my only remaining chance would be to bust out and take it on the run.

Guess she thought three times was enough. I heard her complaining " . . . Sure don't understand. Mis' Sullivan didn't say nothing about going out this morning. How am I supposed to clean up if she ain't home? Maybe she left a key with the janitor. Maybe I should ask him . . . but I ain't got no strength to go

175

chasing around . . . "

She moved away from the door and went padding along the hallway. Then a buzzer sounded in the adjoining apartment.

Moments later I heard a different voice — the voice of a woman who sounded free, white and twice twenty-one. She and black mama tossed the conversation to and fro but I couldn't hear what they were saying. All the same I could guess.

Then the other woman said " . . . Yes, of course. I'm sure everything's all right but it won't do any harm to check. Use my phone and ask him to bring his passkey . . . "

Their voices faded. I knew this was the chance I hadn't hoped to get. Only a few seconds stood between me and a grilling in the sweatbox down at police headquarters.

Yet suddenly I couldn't go. Suddenly I realized there was something I had to do before I left — something I should've done soon as I got my clothes on. It would change the appearance of the whole affair. The law might take a poor view of it but I had bigger worries.

With barely a sound I went back into the cream-and-gold bedroom, unfolded the eiderdown and picked up the dainty doll whose smile now had no more expression than the vacant look in her eyes. She didn't weigh all that much but it was dead weight and carrying her presented quite a problem. I didn't want to drop her and yet neither did I fancy hugging her too close.

And time was breathing down my neck. I had to move fast although I couldn't rush.

Pamela hung in my arms like a sack of bones as I knelt down and laid her gently on the floor beside the bed. Close to her I placed the fluffy mules. On the carpet near her outstretched hand I spread out the wrap.

It looked right. She'd slept in the raw like lots of people do. When she got out of bed to put on her wrap she'd collapsed and died. Whatever the cause of death there were no signs that she hadn't been alone. If I weren't seen leaving her apartment . . .

I shut the bedroom door carefully, tip-toed across the entrance hall and stood listening for a couple of seconds. All I could hear was the daily help's voice mumbling in the next apartment.

As I eased the outer door open, she was saying " . . . OK. Sure . . . just see you ain't long. I'se kinda worried 'cos Mis' Sullivan never done nothing like this before . . . "

She was still talking when I poked my head out and took a quick glance both ways. From end to end the hallway was deserted. The faint whine of the vacuum cleaner had gone. The only sounds were the distant thread of music and the coloured help's peevish voice on the phone.

It took no time at all for me to slide out and pull the door shut. But no time felt like a long time. And the click of the latch sounded like a pistol shot.

With my head bent and my shoulders stooped to reduce my height I walked quickly but quietly towards the elevator. If black mama came out and saw me she wouldn't be able to give much of a description. So long as no one met me face-to-face . . .

No one did. I went past the elevator, pushed through the glass swing doors opening on to the emergency staircase and trotted down the first of steps.

Then the worst was over. Soon as I turned the bend in the stairs I couldn't be seen from up above. By the time the janitor got to the fourth floor and used his passkey to get into apartment 412, I'd be well away.

So I rested a while to take in air and let the pounding in my head settle down. I didn't know how I looked but I knew how I felt. Anybody saw me they'd remember a man who'd acted like he was either drunk or sick.

While I leaned against the wall, breathing in long slow breaths, a relay clicked in the motor-house and the elevator began climbing up from ground level. I didn't need three guesses to know who was in it and where he was heading.

The elevator went past as I trotted downstairs. I heard it stop just about the time I got to the first floor.

There was no one in the lobby but some people came in when I was going out. They didn't give me more than a passing glance. Even if they had good memories, I reckoned their description of me wouldn't amount to much.

On my way to the intersection of Eighty-Fifth and Lexington I looked back more than once. Nobody was tailing me, same as nobody had tailed me to Lakeland Towers. I got an idea the DA's bright young men weren't all that bright . . . or else they'd already been taken off the job . . . although Ed Killick had said they'd be maintaining their stake-out for another twelve hours.

But that had been the night before. Maybe the DA's plans had changed since then. Or maybe Killick didn't know everything.

At the intersection I picked up a cab and rode downtown. It was ten o'clock of a nice crisp morning with the hint of more snow to come but I didn't feel at all crisp. Most of the time I held my head in both hands in case it fell off.

After a while I told myself this was no good. So I got the hackie to drop me at a drugstore.

Three aspirins washed down with a shot of bicarb improved my condition somewhat. Not all at once but pretty soon. When I'd had a cup of hot coffee I felt almost human.

My thought processes began to function better. I realized I must've been concussed to some extent. If I carried on like nothing had happened I might fall down and not get up again. It didn't happen on the movies . . . but I wasn't reading from a movie script.

So I got a Black and White to take me to Brooklyn Hospital and I told an interne in the casualty department that I'd slipped on an icy patch of sidewalk, fallen backwards and banged my head against the wall. I didn't know how long I'd been out.

" . . . But you were for a time completely unconscious?"

"Guess so. I don't remember passing out but coming round was real enough."

"How long ago was this?"

181

"Half an hour . . . give or take."

"Have you had anything to eat or drink in the past half-hour?"

"Aspirin, bicarb and coffee," I said.

He took my temperature, looked in my eyes and checked my reflexes. Then he asked, "Got a headache?"

I said, "That's the understatement of the year."

From there on in the establishment took over. An orderly pushed me in a wheel-chair to the X-ray department where they photographed my head and asked some more questions. Then I was wheeled into a corridor and told to sit there and relax.

The orderly went away. I watched people coming and going, all of them with something to do except me . . . all except me . . . except me . . . except me . . .

Guess I must've dozed off. When I awoke, someone was wheeling me back to Casualty.

This time I was left in a cubicle. I woke up after a while because the interne was asking me if I'd like to see some pretty pictures of my head. The way he asked I reckoned he didn't care a hoot what I liked.

He clipped the photos to a glass screen, switched on a light behind it and stood making reflective noises that weren't meant to mean anything to me. I passed the time seeing mental pictures of a dead doll lying on the floor of her apartment at Lakeland Towers.

Eventually the interne switched off the light and grinned down at me. He said, "Could be worse. There's no fracture of the skull."

I said, "If there's anything worse it shouldn't happen to my worst enemy."

"Not to worry. You'll live. And talking about enemies — " he quit grinning — "you sure you got that lump from banging your head against a wall?"

"I'm not even sure what day it is," I said. "Does it make any difference how I got knocked out?"

"Only to you. The nature of your injury makes me think it might've been caused by a blunt instrument."

The picture in my mind changed to

a shot of a golden girl who'd told me I did too much thinking. I said, "Can you suggest anything more blunt than a stone wall?"

He shrugged and said, "Have it your own way."

"That's right. After all, it's my own head."

"See you take more care of it. Next time — "

"There won't be a next time," I said.

"Good." He unclipped the photos and slid them into an envelope. "Now I'm going to arrange for you to spend at least twelve hours in bed. If you're wise you'll stop there until this time tomorrow morning . . . just to be on the safe side."

It wouldn't have been clever to argue. So I didn't.

Before I was wheeled away, the interne asked, "Anybody you want us to notify where you are?"

That gave me to think the old morbid thoughts. If I didn't live to walk out of hospital it wouldn't matter to a darn soul that I'd gone for keeps. Nobody really cared. A few good-time friends would make the right noises . . . and that was all.

I said, "No. The world can get by without me for one day."

★ ★ ★

Lying in bed was better than walking around. They didn't give me much to eat but that was no cause for complaint. I hadn't much in the way of an appetite.

Most of the time they let me sleep. Most of my sleep was filled with dreams.

Diane Russell featured in all of them — sometimes alone, sometimes with Connie. When they were together I could see them laughing at me and I tried to ask them what was so funny but the words wouldn't come out. Instead someone behind a door asked me why I'd killed a poor coloured woman who'd done me no harm.

Through a growing confusion I protested that a pretty doll had shot Frankie Siccola. I could prove it. If they gave me a chance I could prove it. But everybody was now talking at once and I knew they couldn't hear me.

Then I found myself in a room where a doll was sitting up in bed with her arms held out to me. She had Diane's face but it was Connie's voice that came out of her sweet mouth.

The voice said " . . . *You remind me of Frankie . . . in a sort of way. How about coming around some time? Life's kind of tough for a dame like me . . .* "

Something went off with a bang and I saw the doll lying on the floor with blood running out of its head. Behind the door Diane was saying " . . . *You might get hurt . . . but it's worth dying for a half a million dollars.*"

That dream sequence stuck with me when I awoke late that evening. While I lay thinking about it somebody in a white coat stopped by my bed and asked me if I was feeling better.

I said I'd be fine if I could get a square meal. It seemed like a week since I'd had any nourishment.

He told me I wouldn't starve. " . . . Think

how you'll enjoy breakfast. Has your headache gone?"

"All but. The egg's gone down a lot, too."

"Good. Now, if you'll just lie nice and quiet I'll run the tape over you."

He went through the same routine — eyes, reflexes, temperature — and checked my pulse as a bonus. When he was all through, he said, "I reckon you'll be fit to leave in the morning . . . after breakfast."

"Why can't I go home now?"

"Because it's crowding midnight. What could you do at home that you can't do here?"

It was a good question. I couldn't think of a good answer.

As he left me, he added, "Remember one thing. If you should feel dizzy in the next day or two contact your own doctor without delay. That also applies to noises in the head or visual disturbances . . . in fact, any unusual symptoms. Got that?"

"Loud and clear," I said.

★ ★ ★

Eight o'clock next morning I settled my bill and checked out. For medical attention and all I found it was good value. I reckoned Diane Russell wouldn't have anything to quibble about when she got my list of expenses.

Except for that tender lump on my head I felt OK. It was only when I got home that I didn't feel so good. My keys were missing.

They hadn't been taken by anybody at the hospital. That was for sure. So it was long odds I hadn't had the leather key-case when I took off in a hurry from Lakeland Towers.

Which left me with only one possibility. I didn't need to give myself a headache thinking of any other.

For a minute or two I stood looking at my apartment door while I wondered where I went from here. Then I rummaged through my pockets again as a matter of routine. Last of all I went through the routine of automatically trying the door.

It wasn't locked. That should've surprised me but it didn't. Instead I had the same feeling of menace that had made my short hair prickle when I stood looking into Pamela Connolly's apartment.

No one could have known I'd be back at this hour of the day. Ordinarily I'd have been leaving for the office. If I'd had intruders they wouldn't expect to be interrupted. Neither would they be lying in wait for me.

All the same I had that feeling. I'd ignored it once . . . and I had a lump on my head to prove it.

So I unbuttoned my topcoat, wrapped a hand round the butt of an old friend and turned the doorknob very slowly until it would turn no more. Then I flung the door wide open.

Nothing happened. The door bounced against the wall and swung back a few inches, the sitting-room window rattled momentarily. And that was all. Nothing went on happening.

There was no one in the sitting-room, no sound of anyone anywhere in my flatlet. After a long wary minute I went inside, flipped the door shut behind me and stood listening for another minute.

While I listened I noticed several things. A stranger wouldn't have noticed them but they were quite plain to me. And they all added up to one thing. In the past twenty-four hours I'd had a visitor.

The signs weren't obvious but I could tell. When I'd taken a cautious peek into the bedroom and bathroom I hadn't the slightest doubt. Somebody had frisked the whole place very thoroughly.

I repeated the operation. I didn't think it was necessary but I searched everywhere all the same.

The result was what I'd expected. My possessions were intact. All I'd lost this far was a bunch of keys.

It made a logical pattern. The five one-hundred dollar bills Diane Russell had given me were still in my inside coat pocket. Five Cs hadn't interested the party who'd laid me down to sleep. Five hundred was chicken-feed compared with five hundred thousand.

I didn't need anyone to tell me that

he or she hadn't found what he or she was looking for. And there was only one other place to search. By now he or she would have been and gone. I wondered . . .

8

MY office door wasn't locked. That I had expected. My leather key-case was lying on the desk blotter. I'd expected something like that, too.

The rest was also familiar. I could see traces everywhere of a painstaking search. And if I'd needed confirmation I got it when I opened the desk drawer that had a lock.

The prowler hadn't bothered to lock it but the contents were as tidy as they'd been when I planted the Bible under some papers. My immediate concern was the key that Diane had given me. It was still taped to the underside of the drawer, in the same way and the same position where I'd left it.

Checking the pocket-size Bible was almost a waste of time. I knew what I'd find. And I wasn't disappointed.

As I riffled through the pages until I

came to the Second Book of Samuel I remembered how Diane had leaned over the desk and asked, "*Think anyone would've found it*?"

Her eyes had been laughing at me and she'd looked real pretty. The perfume she'd worn had brought a touch of spring to that chill October day. Its fragrance seemed to linger still.

When I got to page 333 I quit thinking about Diane Russell. The prowler hadn't left empty-handed. My substitute key had gone. Some of the adhesive had gone with it along with a scrap of the page which formed the base of the cavity.

It was all Connecticut to a squeezed orange that I wouldn't get away with the deception for very long. Whoever had the key must also have the letter of authority. A visit to the safe-deposit company would blow my tuck sky-high.

And then . . . The prowler wouldn't need to be a genius to guess I had the genuine key . . . and I now knew my subterfuge had been exposed . . . and I'd be expecting trouble any time from here on in.

All of which depended on whether or not I'd been picked up with a dead doll in that apartment at Lakeland Towers. Somebody would learn pretty soon that I hadn't.

Somebody . . . It had to be Jeff Connolly. He was tailor-made for the part. How he'd found out where Pamela was living presented no problem. He'd forced Siccola to tell him before he put a slug in Frankie's head.

Now he'd squared accounts with both of them. Now all he had to do was get his hands on a parcel of diamonds worth half a million dollars.

It fitted. What I knew and what I could guess almost completed the pattern. Almost . . .

One thing was wrong — a cold fish called Theo Prager. He was bound to have been in on the vault job at Shoemaker Gem Corporation . . . if not in the execution, then at least in the planning. He was Frankie's right hand. He knew the inside secrets of Frankie's organization.

So he must've known a grand jury

194

was about to Investigate Siccola's various rackets. He would also know that Siccola's only hope was to head for distant places and get lost.

Theo Prager, the trusted lieutenant, would know where and when. Loyalty could be stretched too far. Maybe Connie, beautiful golden Connie, was the breaking point.

I was still looking at the open Bible. Odd phrases, a familiar name, passed through my mind without registering as anything more than memories of long ago.

Far back in the past I had learned the story of David and Uriah and a woman called Bath-sheba — a woman whose beauty inspired treachery and murder. As I day-dreamed of a time when the world was young I found myself reading the story again.

. . . *And David arose from off his bed, and walked upon the roof of the king's house: and from the roof he saw a woman washing herself; and the woman was very beautiful to look upon.*

. . . *And David sent and enquired*

after the woman. And one said, Is not this Bath-sheba, the daughter of Eliam, the wife of Uriah the Hittite?

And David sent messengers, and took her; and she came in unto him, and he lay with her . . .

Out of nowhere come a sudden realization that I had only to change the names and this tale of ancient times would have a new meaning for me. It wasn't only kings who betrayed their trust for the sake of a woman.

. . . And David sent to Joab, saying, Send me Uriah the Hittite. And Joab sent Uriah to David . . . And it came to pass in the morning, that David wrote a letter to Joab, and sent it by the hand of Uriah.

And he wrote in the letter, saying, Set ye Uriah in the forefront of the hottest battle, and retire ye from him, that he may be smitten, and die.

And it came to pass, when Joab observed the city, that he assigned Uriah unto a place where he knew that valiant men were.

And the men of the city went out, and

fought with Joab: and there fell some of the people of the servants of David; and Uriah the Hittite died also . . .

. . . And when the wife of Uriah heard that Uriah her husband was dead, she mourned for her husband . . .

It was easy to set the old story in modern dress, all too easy to persuade myself I had only just managed to escape from an apartment where the body of a latter-day Bathsheba had lain naked on the bed. If Frankie had wanted Jeff Connolly's wife he would've arranged it so Connolly wasn't around to object.

That brought me back to Theo Prager. Maybe he had played Joab to Jeff Connolly's Uriah.

But their story had come to a different end. It was the king who had died. And now Bath-sheba was dead.

Events had got out of hand like a play directed by a crazy man. Only Prager was left . . . if I were right.

Unless Frankie had chosen that section of the Bible for his hiding place by chance, I must be right. And it couldn't have been chance. That would've meant believing in the wildest coincidence.

Frankie Siccola had known what he was doing. He always did. Planting the key in the Second Book of Samuel opposite the story of David and Bathsheba would've satisfied Frankie's morbid sense of humour.

It must've been deliberate. The only time he hadn't known what he was doing was when he let somebody with a .45 automatic walk into his room at Duffie's Hotel.

There my thoughts went off at a tangent. Maybe the real answer was in two parts. Maybe one of them was in that last verse.

. . . *And when the wife of Uriah heard that Uriah her husband was dead, she mourned for her husband* . . .

It didn't take strength to pull the trigger of a .45. A woman could've done it — even a dainty doll of a woman like Pamela Connolly. That could've been her idea of mourning . . . when she'd learned that Jeff was dead and who'd arranged to have him killed.

It could have been Pamela who'd taken

a shot at me through the window. Why didn't matter. But one thing for sure was that it hadn't been Pamela who frisked my flatlet and my office.

So there would've had to be two of them — both using a .45. That was asking me to believe in another coincidence. I couldn't and I didn't.

Anyway, thinking round and round in circles wasn't going to get me anywhere. Whoever had taken the phoney key would be coming back for the genuine one. Unless I took care to see I was ready and waiting . . .

My phone rang just as I'd put the Bible away and shut the drawer. A voice I didn't know asked, "Are you Bowman?"

He sounded brusque. I had a notion he was the kind of man who'd always been in the habit of getting his own way.

I said, "I'm Bowman. Who are you?"

"The name's Polk — Herman Polk. Guess you've heard of me."

"Now and again . . . and nothing good."

With no change of voice, he said,

"You've got a helluva gall. People like you don't talk to me that way."

"Wrong. I've just done it."

He took some time to digest that. Then he said in a milder tone, "You're not being very smart. Before you open a big mouth why don't you hear what I have to say?"

For a big operator like Polk to appeal to reason was quite something. I wondered how much ribbing he was prepared to take.

"It won't alter my opinion," I said.

"Your opinion isn't going to keep me awake nights. I called you because I've got a business proposition."

"What makes you think I'd be interested?"

"If you're not you'll be the only shamus on record to pass up an offer of cash money."

I said, "Wrong again. I've turned down your kind of money more than once."

"Waving the banner of freedom could prove expensive," Polk said. "When I want something I'm no tightwad. I pay big."

"How big is big?"

"A down payment of a thousand bucks. That's yours — win, lose or draw. In addition, you get another hundred every day you spend on the job. Is it enough?"

"Depends."

"On what?"

"The goods you're buying," I said.

Polk made a little sound of disapproval. He said, "We'll discuss that when it's just you, me and the four walls."

In a rasping voice, he added, "That's if you can spare an hour of your valuable time, of course."

Anybody paying a thousand dollars for the pleasure of talking to me is entitled to indulge in sarcasm. I said, "I can spare an hour. Know where my office is?"

"Not the foggiest idea. And I don't care a goodgoddamn, either. You think I want to advertise I'm doing business with a private eye?"

"We're not in business yet," I said. "So don't give me the rush act. What you're saying is that you want me to call on you."

"That's right, shamus. Glad I'm getting

201

through. I'll expect you before ten o'clock."

"OK. But don't expect anything else. I'm not committing myself in advance."

"Who's asking you to sign a contract? You say no, so you say no. All you're speculating is a little time."

His voice was receding from the phone as he added, "Don't worry about the cab fare. It's on me."

★ ★ ★

He had an apartment midtown in a respectable middleclass block between Eighth and Ninth. I reckoned that either his neighbours weren't too fussy about the kind of neighbour they had or else Polk owned the whole block.

I used the house phone to tell him I'd arrived. He said I should come on up.

" . . . Carl's been told who you are but not what you are so don't get too gabby."

His apartment was up among the high numbers with an entrance in an alcove at the farthest end of the hallway. The door had just a couple of chrome numerals — no name. Below the numerals there was a bell-push and below that a spyglass.

When I touched the button it made a sound like the tinkling of a silver bell. Something brightened the lens of the spyglass and I guessed I was being carefully inspected. Then the door opened.

He was squat and thick-set with a trunk like an oak tree and powerful arms that were out of proportion to his height. Guess he must've been around five-seven but his width made him look shorter.

Some time in the past he'd taken on all comers in a wrestling booth. He had that kind of face.

And he had the disposition that went with it. In a deep growl, he asked, "You Bowman?"

I said, "Me Bowman."

He jerked his head at me and I went past him and he shut the door. Then he said, "Now I'll have that heater you're carrying inside the waistband of your pants."

"You go jump in the lake," I said.

The expression on his brute face didn't change. After he'd flexed his hands three-four times, he asked, "Want me to take it from you?"

"If you try, I'll bend it over your head."

"That would be a bad mistake."

He wasn't mad at me. It was just a plain statement of fact.

"Look," I said. "I don't aim to stand here trading repartee. Either I keep my gun or I don't keep my date with your boss. Which is it to be?"

His lips drew back against his teeth in a grin like an ape. He said, "I don't make the decisions. I just do as I'm told. And my orders are that no stranger carrying a gun ever gets to see Mr Polk."

"He'll make an exception in my case . . . or else I walk out. Go tell him that."

It took Carl quite a time to make up his mind. At last, he said, "Wait here. And see you don't do any wandering around."

He went through the only other door in the hall and I heard him lock it from the outside. When he'd been gone half a minute I got to wondering about several things.

So I tried the outer door and I found I'd guessed right. It was dead-locked. The release lever wouldn't shift . . . which meant I was imprisoned in a fourteen by twenty cell with an expensive carpet on the floor, an original painting on each of three walls and artistic lighting in all four corners.

The rest of that first minute went by . . . and another minute. I'd just begun to get a feeling of claustrophobia when I heard somebody fiddling with the lock of the inner door.

Carl came back. He said, "It's OK. Mr Polk says you can keep the heater." Whatever his feelings were they didn't show on his battered face.

I followed him across a room with a split-level floor, up a short flight of steps and through a double doorway. By then I'd almost forgotten he was two hundred twenty pounds of domesticated orang-utan in a bulky grey suit.

That was where I slipped up badly.

Carl might not have had much of a mind but what he had was one-track.

We were going through that double door when he stopped dead so I darn near walked into him. And near was enough.

As smoothly as though he'd rehearsed it every day for a year his elbow jerked back with lots of power behind it and slammed me in the pit of the stomach. It felt like the kick of a stallion. All the air gushed out of my lungs and nothing replaced it. I couldn't breathe, I couldn't see. As a KO it was a classic.

If Carl hadn't been there I'd have hit the floor. Like it was all one rhythmic movement he swivelled round, did a neat side-step and slid behind me. His arms clamped mine to my body. Then he began to squeeze.

If he'd wanted he could've cracked half my ribs. Instead he lifted me off the floor and stuck a hand inside my coat so he could get at the Smith and Wesson.

But that was as far as he went. With his mouth close to my ear, he said, "Didn't I say I could take it from you?"

Guess he'd made his point. I was in no state to argue.

When he let me down on to my own two feet I leaned against the doorway and tried to remain alive without air while I massaged the paralysis out of my solar plexus. It wasn't easy, it wasn't quick and it wasn't pleasant.

Carl was in no hurry. While it lasted he stood watching me, his deep-set eyes completely expressionless. I'd have laid long odds he didn't care a damn whether I lived or died.

Soon as my lungs were working again, I said, "That was a helluva thing to do. What if I should tell your boss?"

"He wouldn't fire me if — " Carl grinned humourlessly like an ape again — "if that's what you mean. Mr Polk likes me to have a work-out every so often. Says it keeps me from getting soft. Now let's move . . ."

We crossed another nicely furnished room and stopped at another door. Carl tapped softly with the tips of his fingers, waited a couple of seconds and then told me to go on in.

" . . . I'll be out here all the time. Remember that . . . and keep your nose clean."

One end of the room was all window full of October sky — a few off-white clouds, hazy sunshine, something in the air that comes to New York once in a while. Even the skyline seemed faintly luminous.

A view like that was too good for a character like Herman Polk. Often made me think there was no justice.

Not that he looked a big-time racketeer. His suit, shirt and necktie were expensive but restrained and he had the well-groomed appearance that belongs to the upper crust.

He had an affable manner, too. The smile on his plump face and the twinkle in his nice honest eyes could've got him elected to Congress.

I'd seen him before but I'd never been in his apartment. And for a man with Polk's reputation this room wasn't what I'd have expected.

It had comfortable chairs, an inlaid drinks cabinet and a desk as big as the one Mussolini used so as to boost his ego. All that figured. But I hadn't reckoned on Polk being a patron of the fine arts.

Almost the whole of one wall was filled with books — good books, old leather-bound books, row upon row in sets or single volumes. To collect them must've taken years. Now they represented more than money to a man who could appreciate their real worth.

I wouldn't have thought Herman Polk was that kind of man. Neither would I have imagined he'd have a couple of display cases full of Dresden china and another case crowded with Chinese ivory carvings in every style and design.

Maybe he guessed what I was thinking. Maybe it showed on my face.

He said, "You rated me a peasant . . . eh?" The smile still lingered round his mouth but his eyes weren't laughing.

For someone like me talking with someone like him it was a loaded question. I said, "Don't flatter yourself. Peasants earn an honest living."

Polk tilted back his chair and propped a knee against the edge of the desk. In a quiet voice, he asked, "What gives you the right to criticize how I operate my business?"

"I wasn't exercising a right. I was just answering a damnfool question."

"Why was it a fool question?"

"Because you didn't get me here to ask my opinion of your private hobbies. We were supposed to talk about that offer you made on the phone."

"We'll come to that — " his thoughts and his tongue were on different wavelengths — "soon enough. What's the big rush?"

"Some of us can't afford to waste a morning in idle chit-chat," I said. "We have our bread and cheese to earn."

Without taking his eyes off me he opened a drawer and brought out a bulky envelope. As he tossed it to me, he said, "You'll find a thousand dollars in there. Whether we do a deal or not it's yours. No strings."

"For a thousand bucks you must be buying something," I said.

"Call it the pleasure of your company." His smile came and went almost too fast to register. "Now quit griping about your bread and cheese."

I laid the envelope on his desk. I said, "Before I take your money I want to hear your business offer."

"Didn't I tell you no strings? Stick it in your pocket and don't be a dope."

"Nothing doing. Once it's in my pocket I'll be in yours."

"What're you talking about?"

"You know darn well," I said. "A bribe by any other name still stinks."

Polk leaned farther back and shrugged. He said, "You're crazier than a bed bug. But I'm in an easy-going mood this morning so have it your own way."

"Then let's get down to business."

"OK. Ever heard of a dame called Pamela Connolly?"

The question nearly threw me. But if the look on Polk's face was anything to go by it was a straight question.

I said, "Yes. She's married to Jeff Connolly — the guy who took Shoemaker Gem Corporation for half a million dollars."

"Uh-uh." Polk treated himself to one

of his on-and-off smiles. "You're still in yesterday. As from today, Connolly's a widower."

"How come?"

"She died — that's how."

"You mean someone bumped her off?"

"No, that isn't what I mean. According to my information she just dropped dead."

When I'd allowed enough time, I said, "Guess it's possible. But wasn't she kind of young for that sort of thing?"

"Don't make — " once again Polk was saying one thing and thinking another — "like an inquest. It's how she lived that interests me — not how she died."

He seemed to imagine I knew what he was talking about. I said, "Don't get any idea I'm holding my breath. Alive or dead — I couldn't care less."

"No? You might feel different when I tell you she was living in a swell apartment under a phoney name. Called herself Sullivan."

Polk lowered his chair down on to its front legs. With a subtle change of tone, he asked, "Doesn't that ring a bell?"

Now we'd come to the showdown. I said, "You tell me."

"All right — " there was no longer anything subtle about his tone — "I will. Sullivan was the name Frankie Siccola used when he checked in at that hotel where he was found shot through the head. You've heard of Frankie, haven't you?"

"Yes, I've heard of him. So what?"

"So I happen to know you've been going around asking questions such as how and why and who because somebody wants to pin the rap on Frankie's killer. When I heard what you were up to I became interested."

"Why?"

Little vexed lines pulled down the corners of Polk's mouth. He said, "Don't act the dope. Anything that concerns Frankie's death concerns me."

"Why?"

"You know darn well. Homicide are nursing an idea that I had him eliminated."

"Did you?"

In a voice that was neither too loud nor too defiant, Polk said, "No."

It could've been true. I said, "Then it's no skin off your nose if I poke here and there. What have you got to worry about?"

"Plenty. The longer you keep stirring up this thing, the longer Homicide keep the double-O on my affairs. That cramps my action . . . which cuts down the dividends. I can't afford to have the law prying into my business all the time."

"You can say that again," I said.

"Skip the wisecracks. I want to know what you're going to do about it."

"Nothing. It's too bad if my inquiries embarrass you . . . but that won't make me quit a job I've been hired to do."

With a man-to-man look in his honest eyes, Polk said, "I'm not asking you to quit. It'll take the heat off me if you can prove somebody else put Frankie on ice."

I said, "You're talking two ways at once. Suppose you put your cards on the table and tell me what you really want?"

"All right." He rested a hand on the desk and played piano. "Here it is. If I know what the law is up to I can go carefully in one direction and extend myself in another. That's where you come in."

"How?"

Once again, Polk gave me that true-blue look. Either he didn't know or he didn't care that I'd have trusted him as much as I'd have trusted a second-hand car salesman.

He said, "I'm told you're on pretty good terms with Henderson of the Homicide Bureau and also one of the special investigators working for the DA's office, a persistent guy by the name of Killick. Now useful connections like that — "

"Who told you?"

"I hear things. Would you say what I hear is true?"

"Calling it pretty good terms is an over-statement. We talk to each other . . . and that's about all."

"Talk dealing with the Siccola affair?"

"Mostly. But if you're going to suggest I break confidence by giving you the tip-off you better think again. It's no dice."

Polk quit piano-playing and held up his hand in protest. He looked half shocked and half indignant.

In a pained voice, he said, "Would I ask you to do a thing like that? Would I?"

What griped me was that he knew that I knew he was every kind of double-tongue in the book. I said, "If you thought I'd fall for it — yes."

"Well, you've got it all wrong."

"OK. Sue me for slander."

He tried on a full-dress look of indignation but it didn't fit. He said, "What you don't appreciate is that you're only here because I'm told you always go by the rules. D'you think I don't know the difference between a chiseller and a guy who's on the level?"

It was an old routine. He'd missed with one barrel so now he was trying the other.

I said, "Let's say you do know the difference. Now what's the deal?"

"A straightforward assignment." He pointed to the fat envelope. "That thousand bucks is your retainer."

"For doing what?"

Polk vamped a couple of bars with his left hand. Then he said, "For proving I didn't rub out Frankie Siccola."

There was just the right amount of candour and honesty in his round plump face. Guess he'd been two moves ahead of me from the word go.

I said, "Why chuck your money away? I'm already being paid to find out who pulled the trigger. If it wasn't you, then both jobs will be cleared up for the price of one fee."

"Maybe so. But double money will give you a bigger incentive. And I've already told you the longer this thing is under my feet the more expensive it's going to be. I'm paying you to clean it up fast."

The proposition was kosher. So was the money. No law said I shouldn't take the assignment because I wouldn't believe him if he swore on his mother's life . . . if he'd ever had a mother.

It didn't matter how I felt — except to me. And I had a latent feeling that stringing along with Herman Polk might show another sort of dividend.

Guess he knew it was just talk when I said, "You don't need to hire your own law. The Siccola killing is under investigation by both Homicide and the DA's office. They can get results that I could never get . . . and you'll have what you want for free."

He got rid of Honest Joe and gave me a look of exasperation. He said, "Are you kidding? The law doesn't care a damn who blasted Frankie Siccola . . . unless somebody hands them proof that I organized it. I know I didn't. So they'll go through the movements without really trying until I've got a long grey beard."

There he placed both hands on the desk and pushed himself to his feet. Then he added, "I want results PDQ and I'm willing to pay for them. If you have any objections I'll get myself another boy. If not, pick up your retainer and get the hell out of here."

I put the envelope in my pocket. I said, "For years I hated Frankie Siccola's guts. But he sure did me a great big favour when he got himself sewed in a blanket.

It's been a real shot in the arm for business."

A changed look came into Polk's face. He said, "I'm not complaining, either . . . if I can get the law out of my hair. What was your beef with Siccola — a woman?"

"No, nothing like that."

Polk looked like he didn't believe me but it wasn't important. He said, "I don't go for dames the way some guys do. That's where me and Frankie were different. He couldn't live without them."

In my mind there was a composite photograph in the shape of a three-leaf clover — Pamela and Connie and Diane. It was faded with age like a picture of women long dead.

I said, "If he could've done, he might've lived a lot longer. People often used to say women would be the death of him."

"Maybe they were," Polk said.

He waited until I reached the door before he added, "There's something in the Talmud about guys like Frankie

Siccola. As near as I can remember it says a man who talks too much with women becomes foolish. Guess those old boys knew a thing or two."

"Guess so," I said. "All the same, it might not have been Frankie but one of his women who talked too much. I'll give you a buzz when I've got any news . . ."

Carl was parked outside, his feet wide apart, his long arms dangling. Without saying a word he turned and led me back along the return route to the hallway door.

When he'd unlocked it he half-turned to look at me with no expression on his battered face. He said, "As you was coming out of Mr Polk's room I heard you mention somebody called Frankie and I wondered if it could be Frankie Siccola you'd been talking about."

"It could be," I said. "It could also be Frankie Frisch, Frank Sinatra or Franklin Delano Roosevelt. What else did you pick up while you were flapping a big ear?"

Inside his bull head he chewed it over slowly and methodically. Then he said,

"I wasn't listening-in. I just couldn't help hearing his name . . . and it's my job to look out for Mr Polk."

"What connection has he got with Frankie?"

"None at all . . . except that Siccola was in the same line of business. And I aim to see nobody creeps up behind Mr Polk with a gun. If I'd been carrying iron for Siccola it wouldn't have happened."

"If Theo Prager couldn't stop it what makes you think you could've done any better?"

"Maybe — " Carl opened the hallway door and flapped a hand to shoo me out — "maybe Prager didn't try."

"Meaning what?"

The door began to close. Through the narrowing gap, Carl gave me one of his toothy grins.

He said, "Meaning somebody should ask Prager where he was the night somebody turned the heat on Frankie Siccola . . . "

9

AROUND noon I stopped by at police HQ and handed the desk sergeant a sealed envelope containing the .45 slug that had made a hole in my living-room window. When Henderson got it he'd know what it was and what was to be done with it.

Twelve-fifteen I called in at a dinette and stoked up. One o'clock I went back to the office.

No one had tailed me from my office to Herman Polk's apartment. No one had tailed me from there to police HQ . . . or to the dinette . . . or back to square one again. That was puzzling. Just a little puzzle but it gave me to think.

With my feet up on the desk I lounged in my old familiar chair and went on thinking for the best part of an hour. I'd arrived at certain tentative conclusions by the time the phone rang.

Henderson asked, "Where were you all yesterday?" He made it sound like we'd had a date and I'd stood him up.

"Here and there," I said.

"Well, here wasn't your office and there wasn't your flatlet. I tried both places during the day and also late in the evening."

"Maybe I'd just gone out each time you phoned."

"Possible . . . but when I finally gave up it was kind of late. Didn't you sleep at home last night?"

"That's a personal question I'm not going to answer. What's it got to do with you where I was or where I slept?"

In a dour voice, he said, "After the events of the night before last I see no reason why I shouldn't keep tabs on you."

"Worried in case something might happen to me?"

"Unofficially, my only worry is that something might not. Officially, I have to treat you as though you were a civilized member of society."

"You say the nicest things," I said.

"Don't mention it. Tell me instead why you handed over that .45 shell and then dashed off. Scared you wouldn't be allowed to leave?"

"No, I was hungry and I thought I'd grab a bite to eat. Meeting you first would've put me off my food. Anyway, why this great urge to speak with me?"

"I had some news that should interest you. It's twenty four hours old now so it'll keep another couple of minutes. I got Ballistics to run a comparison check on that slug you dug out of your living-room wall and the result was exactly what I'd expected."

"Same gun," I said.

"Beyond any doubt. That means it's almost certain to have been the same finger on the trigger."

"Almost isn't good enough. Lay me better than evens and you got yourself a bet."

"Are you saying it could've been two different people?"

"No. I'm just not buying your proposition

224

with my eyes shut. What was your first piece of news?"

There a midget Donald Duck cut in on our wire. When it cleared, Henderson said, "We've found Jeff Connolly's wife, Pamela."

"Where?"

"In a ritzy apartment uptown. Place called Lakeland Towers. Know it?"

That sort of question had to be defused before it was safe to handle. My only other risk was that some day Polk might mention our conversation.

I said, "I'm not in the habit of visiting with people who live in ritzy apartments. What did Mrs Connolly have to say for herself?"

"Nothing."

"Do you mean — " I only hoped Henderson would never learn I'd made a monkey out of him — "that you couldn't get her to talk?"

"Neither could anybody else. She was dead."

My next question was the one I'd asked Herman Polk. He hadn't been able to give me the answer I needed but there was a good chance Henderson would know by now.

I said, "How had she died?"

"Not by violence . . . at least, not in the sense you and I understand it. The autopsy report says death was due to vagal inhibition. Does that convey anything to you?"

"Yes, I've read about it somewhere. Happens in cases of shock as when people fall into the water and are found dead but not from drowning. Women have also died when they were gripped by the neck although the pressure wasn't enough to cause strangulation."

Henderson said, "You should give a lecture on the subject. In this case there were very faint bruises under the skin of her throat but they hardly prove anything either way. No sign of a struggle or that there'd been an intruder in the apartment."

"Any sign of her husband?"

"No. None of her immediate neighbours had ever seen him. I'm not surprised, either."

"Why?"

"Because the circumstances indicate he'd never been there. She hadn't been known by her real name. People knew her as Mrs Sullivan . . . which brings us right back to an old friend of yours, doesn't it?"

"Another one of Frankie Siccola's women," I said.

"Nothing surer. If Diane Russell was telling you the truth about that Shoemaker Gem Corporation heist — "

"It was you who wouldn't believe it."

"Things have happened since then. Now we know Pamela and Frankie were sharing a love-nest at Lakeland Towers, it changes the whole complexion of what took place at Duffie's Hotel."

"You think it was Connolly who did the shooting?"

"He had a darn good motive," Henderson said. "Sharing half a million dollars was one thing but sharing his wife was a different kettle of fish."

"So your idea is that he came out of his hidey-hole and put a slug in Frankie. Then he laid low for a while. When the time was right he came back again, called on his wife and scared her to death. Is that it?"

"Well, as a working theory it's feasible if nothing more."

"Except for one flaw," I said. "How did Connolly find out his wife was living at Lakeland Towers?"

"Could be — " Henderson wasn't in a hurry to commit himself — "could be somebody told him."

"Who told the somebody? And before you answer that, how did the somebody know where to contact the elusive Jeff Connolly?"

Henderson said, "I'm beginning to think you're asking questions that are the wrong questions and you've thought out the right ones. In other words, it wasn't Connolly at all."

"Not the way it looks to me."

"Then who?"

Now I was like a man running downhill and travelling so fast he couldn't stop. I said, "Some John Doe or Jane Doe who knows what transpired between Connolly and Frankie Siccola after the gopher job at Shoemaker Gem Corporation."

"We've already got a pretty good notion of what happened. Connolly disposed of Mike Tew and then he split the take with Siccola."

"All this wasn't staged in Madison Square Garden," I said. "How do we know there was any split?"

Once again Henderson was in no hurry to jump in with both feet. At last, he said, "That's giving this business a brand-new slant. Suppose you go on from there?"

"No, not yet. I've got nothing more than a hunch. If it checks out I'll tell you."

"See you do. It might not be healthy to play this hand close to the chest. You've already had a lucky break so don't push your luck."

The tender spot on my head gave a little throb to remind me of something he didn't know about. I said, "You're preaching to the converted."

"OK. Keep in touch. Now if you're all through — "

"Just one thing more. I read the story about Mike Tew but I didn't pay much attention at the time. What was the name of the place where he was found dead?"

"Reedsville's the nearest spot on the map. It's some miles west of Newburgh. Tew and Connolly had a fishing lodge they'd visited off and on for two-three months before the Shoemaker job. They bought supplies from Reedsville — a one-horse town without the horse — so the locals had got used to seeing them around."

"How did people discover what had happened?"

"Some kids went fishing. On their way past the lodge one of them took a peek in at the window and saw Tew lying on the floor. He'd been shot in the back of the head."

"What calibre of gun?"

Henderson said, "Not a .45 . . . if that's what you're thinking. Killed the same way as Frankie Siccola but this was a .22."

"Could've been the type that's small enough to be carried in a woman's purse," I said.

"No strange woman had been seen in the neighbourhood. Besides, the tip-off we'd had was that Connolly and Tew had worked together on the Shoemaker job . . . and Connolly was missing along with the stolen diamonds."

"Which made it all fit very neatly."

"It still does," Henderson said. He didn't sound too sure.

"They'd always arrived by car, I suppose?"

"Yes. And, as you'd expect, that had gone, too."

"As you'd expect," I said.

Guess he didn't like the way I said it. In a resentful voice, he asked, "What're you griping at? Why don't you say what you have in mind?"

"Because it's only a hunch — if that. Did anyone see the pair of them arrive on that last occasion?"

"They wouldn't ordinarily be seen. A mile or so from Reedsville there's a turn-off along a dirt track leading to the fishing lodge. The only time local people knew Connolly and Tew were at the lodge was when one or other of them came into the general store for supplies. And before you say — "

"I wouldn't dream of it," I said. "All I'm saying right now is — so long."

★ ★ ★

When I'd made arrangements by phone to pick up a rented car, I rang Diane Russell's number. It was merely a gesture. I'd taken her money and I had to show some sign of life.

If she wasn't home, so much the better. I could always say I'd called a couple of times and got no reply.

As it happened, she answered before the bell had rung twice. She said, "I've been expecting to hear from you today. Made any progress?"

I said, "Only in a negative kind of way. Someone ran the tape over my office yesterday while I was elsewhere. The party in question was looking for that key you gave me."

Diane seemed to be another one who wasn't in a hurry. She took plenty of time before she asked, "They didn't get it, I hope?"

"No, it's quite safe. But they took

232

a substitute key I'd stuck inside the Bible."

"Was that — " she hesitated and began again — "was that a good idea? They're bound to find out pretty soon they've been tricked."

"Then it'll be interesting to see what they do next," I said.

"Yes . . . but I think you shouldn't have let them find any key at all. This way you might be asking for trouble unnecessarily."

"I don't need to ask for it. I've already had a sample. Night before last someone took a shot at me through my living-room window."

That made her go quiet for an even longer spell. Then she said uneasily, "Perhaps it had nothing to do with the — the business we discussed."

"Oh, but it had. There isn't a shadow of doubt."

"You could be wrong. How did anyone know I'd hired you to investigate Frankie's death?"

"I've been asking myself the same question."

"But this attempt on your life must've happened only a few hours after I called at your office. And you shouldn't need me to tell you I never mentioned it to a soul."

I said, "Maybe I shouldn't need . . . but I'm glad to hear you say it. And I'd advise you not to open your door unless you know who's outside. Some people seem to have access to confidential information."

After another pause, Diane said, "It's — it's frightening. I wouldn't blame you if you wanted to back out."

Her tone didn't match her words. I knew she'd call me every kind of yellowbelly if I suggested throwing in my hand.

So I said, "Too late for that now. Whoever's gunning for me wouldn't know I'd quit. Besides, I'd like to help you see this through — and not just for the money."

"That's — that's really nice of you."

Her voice made me think of the perfume she wore. I could almost imagine she was smiling her warm sweet smile. As I told her goodbye I told myself it might be fun if we got together some time. It just might . . .

★ ★ ★

The phone rang as I was getting into my topcoat. For a moment I felt tempted to let it ring. Maybe it would've been better in the long run if I had. But I didn't.

I was glad, too, when I heard Connie's sugarplum voice. She said, "Didn't you promise to stop by one of these nights?"

"Sure . . . and I haven't forgotten."

"Well, how about tonight? I feel kinda lonely."

"Sorry, but I can't make it. Suppose I give you a ring tomorrow or the day after and we'll fix up a date?"

"Don't call us, we'll call you," Connie said. "You allergic to me or something?"

I said, "You couldn't be more wrong. I'm just not free tonight."

"If that's the truth — " she'd gone all little-girl sad — "guess there's nothing I can do about it."

Somebody like me could never lie to somebody like Connie. I said, "Let's say it's half the truth."

"All right. Now give me the other half."

"Don't you know yourself? I'm not the kind of guy you think I am."

"What's that supposed to mean? You look like the right kind of guy and you behave like the right kind of guy. Any other way I can tell the difference between you and all the bums I've known?"

"That's the trouble," I said. "There is no difference. You can't trust me any more than you could trust them."

She laughed — just a little laugh that could've meant anything or nothing. She said, "Like I told you a couple of times already, you think too much."

"Maybe. But it might not be a bad idea if you did some thinking."

That rated another little bubbling laugh. Then she asked, "Have you been kidding yourself I didn't know what was going on inside your head when you were here Monday night?"

If ever I'd had an invitation served up on a silver platter this was it. I said, "You don't seem able to make up your mind. Didn't you say you were all through with men? After you heard about Frankie you weren't — "

"Frankie was different. He never asked — he took. But if I like you and you like me — well, is there a law against it or something?"

That old, old man in my subconscious went into his old, old routine while I was trying to think of a way to say no when I wanted to say yes.

. . . It's just over a week since Frankie Siccola walked out of his home on Riverside Drive and the marital delights that went with it. Only a couple of days since his wife and you and a handful of others watched two grave-diggers toss dirt in his face. Only a couple of days . . . Yet already she's saying there's a spare pillow in her bed again. That Russell woman wasn't far wrong when she called her a cheap tramp . . .

The old man wasn't far wrong, either. Connie might look like a golden princess but looks weren't everything. All she had to offer was fun in bed. And for that looks weren't necessary when the lights were out.

Now Diane had what Connie lacked — Diane had character. Maybe it wasn't altogether virtuous character but the good and the bad combined to make her a person.

One thing they shared. Both of them had slept with Frankie Siccola. But I wasn't Frankie.

Meanwhile Connie was making sweet talk on the phone. And whether I'd say yes or no was still an even-money bet.

So I said, "You're right. There isn't any law against it. But business comes before pleasure . . . and I have to go out of town. I was just leaving when you rang."

Her voice went a trifle flat. Like little-girl disappointed, she asked, "Is that the polite brush-off?"

I said, "No, it's on the level."

"When d'you think you'll be back?"

"Depends how I make out."

"Is this connected with what happened to Frankie?"

"Indirectly — yes. At least, I hope so. But you never can tell."

That was as much as was good for her to know. Any more might not have been good for me.

Guess it was enough. She quit prying. Instead she switched back to the birds and the bees.

She said, "If you don't call me by weekend, I'll know it's because you think I got no class."

"Don't be crazy," I said.

Whatever she was, whatever she'd been, I couldn't put the skids under her. She'd already been hurt enough for one lifetime.

Maybe I wanted to let her down gently because of what she'd been through or maybe I was giving myself a putty medal. The truth might've been that she'd got under my skin.

Now all I know is that I added, "Whenever I can grab some time off, I'll call you. That's a promise."

Connie said, "Make it soon. And mind how you go . . . "

10

MID-AFTERNOON traffic wasn't so bad that it couldn't have been worse. I made fair time getting clear of the City limits. When I hit the Newburgh highway I put my foot down.

It was another chilly day and the forecast was that there would be a moderate to severe frost by nightfall. I was glad the Mustang had an efficient heater.

Under a grey sky I headed north. Englewood . . . Piermont . . . Haverstraw . . . Highland Falls . . . I ran into a belt of rain and sleet as I cleared the suburbs of Cornwall.

A mile or so farther on a minor road forked off the main highway. There was a signpost pointing north-west — *REEDSVILLE* — *7 miles*.

By then the sleety rain had become much heavier and premature dusk was setting in. On either side of the winding road an occasional tree — naked and solitary — stood out against the gloomy sky. I began thinking I'd chosen a bad day to take a ride in the country.

Soon I caught sight of the two and a half streets that made up Reedsville. Moments later I came to another side road forking left. This one was unmade and barely wide enough for a single car. I reckoned it must be the dirt track that Henderson had talked about.

It twisted and turned through a patch of woodland choked here and there with overgrown bushes until the trees thinned out near the shores of a small lake. There the shoestring ended. Where it petered out a trail curved past the lake to a wooden shack raised above ground level on log piles.

There was no sign of life anywhere. I could hear only the rain slanting down on the barren trees. Out on the lake the surface frothed and steamed under the downpour.

I took a wrench and a screwdriver from the trunk, locked up the car and sprinted

241

from the bridle path with ice-cold rain driving in my face. By the time I got to the shack my shirt collar was wet and clammy.

A couple of steps led up to the door. It had an uncurtained window on either side and a crude sort of porch that kept me from getting soaked while I went to work on the lock.

To begin with I tried finesse but that got me nowhere. So I used the screwdriver to gouge a space between the door-frame and the leading edge of the door. Then with the handle of the wrench I forced back the upright until the tongue of the lock sprang free.

Inside the shack there wasn't much in the way of furniture: two camp beds, a bare wooden table, a couple of chairs, a kerosene stove, a lantern hanging from the rafters, some cups and plates and cutlery and canned stuff in a closet. Apart from odds and ends that was about all. It looked as though Tew and Connolly had reckoned on buying their other needs from the general store in Reedsville.

The lamp had a full reservoir of

kerosene. I found a bottle of alcohol for heating the mantle burner and got the thing going. Pretty soon it was giving me ample light to search the whole place — walls, rafters and floor.

I did it twice before I convinced myself I'd come a long way to no purpose. The result was negative. If there hadn't been a reddish-brown stain on one of the floorboards I'd have thought this was the wrong fishing lodge.

Must've been about then that my thoughts began to stray in another direction. When I'd checked the stove I was sorry I hadn't asked Henderson to come along.

It was the kind that would keep the shack warm and also provide a hob on top for one-pan cooking. Like the lantern, the reservoir was full.

So they'd had the means to fix themselves some coffee and do simple chores like heating a can of beans or soup or boiling water for instant mashed potato. But they hadn't used either lamp or stove on their last visit to the fishing lodge.

I went outside, walked right round the shack and came in again. All I got was wet. There was no can anywhere, inside or out — no can that Connolly or Tew should've had for a reserve supply of kerosene.

I could think of one explanation that fitted the circumstances. When I'd studied it from every angle I decided it was the only explanation.

The second last time they'd spent a weekend at the shack they had filled both lantern and stove with kerosene before they left. On their way back to New York they'd stopped off at the store in Reedsville and handed in the reserve can for re-filling.

Maybe the idea had been to pick it up on their return. Maybe they'd have collected it when they called in for supplies. Maybe anything. It didn't matter. What did matter was that they hadn't used stove or lamp at all . . . or hardly at all.

Logically, that meant only one thing. What had happened at the shack must've taken place almost as soon as they

244

arrived. Tew had been shot dead . . . Jeff Connolly had gone off in a great big hurry . . .

The noise of the rain lashing down on the roof formed a background to my thoughts. If I told Henderson he'd say I wasn't telling him anything he didn't already know. And he'd be right, at that.

In the spread of light from the hanging lantern I stood looking down at the dirty brown stain where Mike Tew had fallen when he got a .22 slug in the head. Just like Siccola. And the link between both of them had been Jeff Connolly.

I squatted on my haunches and studied the irregular mark on the bare wooden floor. It reminded me of a map of England except that it was cut off on the eastern side from the Wash to Beachy Head where the blood had stopped at a joint between two floorboards.

It didn't seem to have any special significance until I checked the other joints. Then I got the idea it might mean something.

The spreading blood hadn't stopped

where the two boards joined. It had run down into the crack because the joint didn't fit properly. Neither did the joint one board farther away from the bloodstain. That fifteen-inch floor-board fitted less tightly than any of the others.

I moved the table out of the way, unhooked the hanging lamp and stood it beside me on the floor. Then I made use of the screwdriver again.

The board wasn't easy to shift but I managed to prise it up at last. When I'd pushed it clear, I lowered the lantern down into the gap between two of the joints.

All I could see was earth several feet below the floor. Farther off the light showed me some of the piles on which the shack was supported.

From up above that was all there was to see. With the lantern dangling in one hand and the screwdriver in the other I let myself down through the gap until my feet touched the ground.

It was softer ground than I'd expected. Soon as I'd done some poking with the screwdriver and used my hands as scoops I found out why.

A man's topcoat had been buried just below the surface. It lay flat and neatly folded so that it occupied less space than if it had been rolled up in a bundle.

The next thing I uncovered was a grey homburg. There were tiny holes in the sweatband where somebody's initials had been fastened . . . just the holes. With the noise of the rain all around me I dug deeper still.

My hands became numb from the cold damp earth. As I went on burrowing hurriedly like a dog in search of a bone something with many legs scuttled between my fingers and made my skin creep.

If I'd had any kind of spade it would've been easy. I'd have been able to excavate the whole length of the trench. Instead I concentrated on the end where I'd found the grey homburg, the end where I'd started. It seemed the right place to choose.

It was. In another minute or so I'd removed the soft earth to a depth of several inches below the spot where the hat had lain. And a moment later I knew I didn't need to make any more like a dog.

As I cleared away the final layer of dirt I exposed a handkerchief. Before I lifted it out of the shallow cavity I could guess what I'd find . . . and what I could guess chilled me with a greater cold than the sleet and the blustering wind.

The handkerchief had been used to cover the face of a man — a horribly bloated and discoloured face with bulging eyes and tongue protruding from his mouth like a mottled balloon. In the light of the lamp I saw enough in one brief look to know he'd been dead many weeks. It took a long time for a body to reach that advanced stage of decomposition.

One look was all that my stomach could tolerate. With shaky hands I laid the handkerchief over his face again.

Then a sudden driving urge took possession of me like the fear in one of my childhood dreams. Darkness increased that fear when I'd reached up through the hole in the floor and put the lantern out of harm's way.

I had a bad time in the next few seconds. The stench of putrefaction began to choke me. As I heaved myself up into the shack in frantic haste I'd have sworn that nameless things were about to drag me down to that place of death and corruption.

It would've been a useless exercise to replace the floor-board. All I desperately wanted was to get away.

So I hung the lamp on its hook suspended from the rafters, released the pressure valve in the kerosene tank and went outside before the shadows ganged up on me. Then I used the wrench to lever the tongue of the lock back into its socket.

Last of all I rubbed earth on the chipped edge of the door-frame and the door. Those kids from Reedsville might come snooping again . . . and I reckoned it would be as well if no one disturbed the man who'd been buried in a shallow grave under the floor.

The rain had slackened and the sky was

clearing a little. I walked back to the car, wiped the rough dirt off my hands with a rag and sat for a while looking at the shack where two men had died because of one man's greed.

A glimpse of late afternoon sunshine sparkled on the dripping trees as I drove slowly along the unmade road to the fork that led to Reedsville. When I got there I thought of calling Henderson from a pay station or the village store but I decided against it.

Time enough to tell Henderson after I got back to town. There was no rush. The man who'd been rotting for weeks under the floor of the shack wouldn't go for a walk before the law arrived.

* * *

I wasn't required to make a return journey to the fishing lodge. Homicide took a statement, asked a few supplementary questions and told me I'd be called to give evidence at the inquest. Then they turned me loose.

Henderson was nowhere around while

I was at the Bureau. I reckoned his whereabouts were none of my business so I didn't poke my nose into his business.

A more pressing concern was that I hadn't eaten since midday. I was hungry, dirty and tired. But dirty came first. The feel of that mouldering earth made me want to throw up.

An hour in a turkish bath helped a lot. Half an hour's feeding completed the treatment. Now I wasn't all that tired.

All the same I went home to my two-roomed walk-up, stripped and showered and changed from necktie to shoes. After that I felt much better.

A shot of medicinal bourbon didn't do any harm, either. Then I dialled the number of an over-furnished house on Riverside Drive.

There was no reply. So I poured out another inch of medicine. While I was sipping it, my phone rang.

Ed Killick said, "I've just heard the news. Do you know who the dead guy was?"

The way he put it sounded wrong. I said, "Are you asking me or telling me?"

"I'm asking you. All I've been told is that he had a bullet hole in the back of his head. This far Homicide haven't managed to identify him."

"If he isn't Jeff Connolly then I'm Uncle Mao," I said.

"Well, Connolly's the obvious choice but it's going to be a darn tough job to identify the body. They say nobody could recognize its face."

"What they say is right. It would scare the wits out of those guys who make horror movies."

"I'm not surprised. If it is Connolly he's been buried there since the day they skipped town after the robbery at Shoemaker Gem Corporation. Looks like there must've been three members of that gopher mob."

"And the third man scooped the jackpot," I said.

"Yeh. Got any ideas?"

"Nothing concrete. But I'm working on it."

"Me, too. If you come up with something will you tell me . . . or pass it on to your pal Henderson?"

"He's no pal of mine," I said. "Time you got that into your noodle. I've known him since 'way back when — that's all."

"OK. Don't act like I'd insulted you. Henderson's not a bad guy. Although he and I haven't always hit it off, he rates pretty high with me."

I said, "Mazeltov. I hope you're both very happy. Now do you mind transferring your chit-chat to somebody else's phone? I've got a call to make."

"Business . . . or personal?"

If I hadn't liked Ed I'd have told him where he could go. I said, "Could be a bit of each."

"Is the business related to this afternoon's business out at Reedsville?"

"Sure. What else would it be?"

In a changed voice, Ed asked, "Will you go all hot under the collar if I offer you some advice?"

Most people who give me their advice for free mean well. I said, "Save your breath. You're going to tell me to mind my step. I've been told the same thing once today already."

"All right, I won't — " he was trying

to sound off-hand — "I won't bore you. Guess you're old enough to look out for yourself . . . although playing the loner in an affair of this kind isn't exactly adult."

"I've always been a loner. And if you're thinking of the shot that missed me, forget it. I won't set myself up as a target again. Once is one time too many."

Ed Killick said, "As it happens that's what I was thinking of. Funny business, wasn't it?"

"Not from where I was standing. Couple or three inches nearer and my brains would've made a mess of the living-room carpet."

"If you've got any brains . . . and use them."

Something about the way he said it triggered off a new response in my mind. I said, "Just what are you driving at?"

"That shot from the street. Haven't you wondered how the party outside came to miss? You were a stationary target with the light behind you."

"True enough. But with so many other

things happening I haven't given it much thought."

"Maybe you should."

"It would save time if you came across with the answer you've arrived at," I said.

"Nothing doing. I don't go for a one-way trade. You've got to give if you want to receive."

"Such as what?"

"The result of that phone call you're going to make soon's I hang up."

They say a fair deal shouldn't be turned down unless there's something better. I had no prospects of anything better.

So I asked Ed where he'd be in the next hour or thereabouts. He said he'd stop at the office until he heard from me.

" . . . I've sent out for a sandwich and a cup of coffee. Got enough work here to keep me busy from now till tomorrow."

"Then I'll call you around nine o'clock," I said.

★ ★ ★

The next time I rang Connie's number she answered the phone herself. She said, "Say, that's pretty quick. Didn't you go outa town after all?"

"Yes, I've been there and back. Got in about a couple of hours ago. I phoned you twice but there was no reply."

"Oh, I'm real sorry about that. I went on a shopping binge this afternoon and then I treated myself to a facial. After that I had a meal in a classy place off Fifth and . . . well, I can't be expected to stay home for the rest of my life just because now I'm a widow . . . "

Before I could break in she ran on, " . . . Say, you know what? I ain't never been a widow before. Makes me feel old and wrinkled. You think I am?"

I said, "I shouldn't have to tell you what I think. So don't fish for compliments."

"It's nice to hear them — " her voice was like molasses — "all the same. You calling on me this evening?"

"Not the way I'm fixed right now. I

256

told you I wouldn't be free until weekend. Incidentally, where's your help?"

"Don't tell me you've taken a shine to fat-and-ugly."

"Never mind," I said. "All I wanted to know was why she didn't answer the phone while you were — "

"Don't be grouchy. I was only kidding. As it happens I've given her notice to quit and she took the half-day off to go looking for another job. That's why there was nobody home. Now can we talk about something else?"

"Sure. I'd like to know where I can locate Theo Prager."

Connie seemed to lose her desire for talk. She took plenty of time before she asked, "Why? What d'you want with him?"

"A mouth-to-mouth conversation on a subject of mutual interest."

She said, "That's jibber-jabber to me. What's it sound like in English?"

"He'd understand," I said. "Have you spoken with him recently?"

"Only once. He stopped by after the funeral to ask how I was making out.

Told me if I needed a shoulder to lean on I could use one of his. Wasn't that nice of him?"

I said, "Real nice. If you've got his number tell him I might be willing to do a deal. Will you do that?"

"Whatever you say. But I didn't know you two were acquainted."

"Lots of things you don't know. Some other time I'll explain what it's all about."

With no resentment in her voice, she said, "You treat me like I was still in kindergarten."

"That's because I don't see why you should think too much. Don't you always say that's my big fault?"

"Guess so." Her tone became milk-and-honey again. "You could get me to do most things if you asked right."

I said, "Well, now I'm asking you to call Prager and tell him I've been wondering where he was when Connolly and Tew took a powder after the Shoemaker robbery. You can also say I haven't talked with anybody else yet. Got all that?"

Connie repeated it almost word for

word. " . . . You lost me a long way back but I suppose he'll understand."

"He will," I said. "And if he wants to give me a ring, I'll be home all evening."

11

BETWEEN eight-fifteen and eight-thirty I checked the Smith and Wesson twice. Twenty minutes off nine I checked it again. After that I twiddled my thumbs and sat hating myself because I'd packed up smoking.

Close on nine o'clock I was stretching my legs when the phone bell jolted me to a halt. I let it ring a few times until I'd got my breath back before I lifted the receiver.

A voice I didn't know said, "This is Theo Prager. You got something to say to me?"

He sounded like he looked — not quite human. If a mountain cat could talk it would have had Prager's voice.

I said, "If you're interested in a proposition."

"What kind of proposition?"

"The kind that might save the seat of your pants from getting toasted."

"You make noises that don't make sense," Prager said. "Your message said something about a robbery. Sure you got the right guy?"

"Until you phoned me I couldn't be sure — but I am now," I said.

He didn't need time to think. With him reaction was instinctive.

In the same flat monotone, he asked, "When are you going to come to the point?"

"We've come to it. This afternoon a partner of yours turned up — somebody by the name of Jeff Connolly whom the law has been hunting for the past couple of months."

"You're nuts. I've got no partner of that name."

"Not any more," I said. "The only partner he's got now is the guy in the next icebox down at the morgue."

"What makes you think this has anything to do with me?"

"There's a simple answer to that. I'm the one who found him buried under the fishing lodge out Reedsville way."

For only as long as it would've taken

261

me to count off five seconds, Prager kept quiet. Then he asked, "How d'you know it's Jeff Connolly?"

"Same as I know it was you who knocked him off. I'm pretty sure you disposed of Mike Tew as well . . . but I can't prove that."

"You can't prove anything," Prager said. "If this is a shakedown, you picked the wrong customer."

I said, "The first part scores a bull. It is a shakedown. And you either split the Shoemaker gems fifty-fifty or I'll tie the rap round your neck so tight you'll roast like a Thanksgiving turkey. You can hang up if you don't believe me."

He didn't hang up. Playing poker over the years had cost me plenty but it had also taught me plenty.

Without the slightest hesitation, he said, "For the sake of another dime I can afford to see you. What've you got?"

"Something you left behind that day when you dropped Connolly's body through the hole in the floor — something that links you and him together more closely than the marriage vows in church.

262

With you, death hasn't brought any parting. He's tied to you like a Siamese twin."

Maybe Prager bought it lock, stock and barrel. Maybe not. How he felt didn't show in his voice.

He asked, "What is this something I left behind?"

"You shouldn't need me to tell you."

"Oh, but I do, I do. Seeing I've never heard of a place called Reedsville and I've never been to this fishing lodge you talk about, don't you think I'm entitled to a bit more than this load of guff?"

That was a lot of talk for a normally taciturn character. I reckoned he didn't consider he was in a normal situation.

I said, "All you're entitled to is your half of a two-way split."

"One half of zero won't pay the rent. I don't know a darn thing about the Shoemaker heist."

"Too bad. I was relying on it to provide for my old age."

"Old age is what a shyster private eye doesn't see. Small-time players shouldn't try to muscle in on the major league."

"Famous last words," I said. "Yours. If anything happens to me what I've got will be handed to the DA within twenty-four hours."

"Nothing's gonna happen to either of us."

"If you'll back that with real money I'll lay any odds you like that pretty soon you'll be playing the leading role in a barbecue up at the Big House."

Prager said, "Turn that disc over. It's getting kinda monotonous. I didn't rub out Connolly or anyone else so I know you're bluffing."

"You'd change your tune if you saw the little souvenir I picked up this afternoon. Suppose we get together and I show you?"

Once again he didn't need to take time out for thought. Guess he'd planned the final move before he called me.

He said, "That should be a barrel of fun. Where and when?"

"Here and now," I said.

"Not a chance. How do I know what you've got laid on for me? We'll meet some public place or not at all."

"OK with me. You name it."

This time he was just a little too quick. It didn't register with me like it should because I was just a little too slow.

He said, "Subway station on Broadway and East Fourteenth in half an hour. Right?"

"I'll be there," I said.

Soon as he hung up I checked the Smith and Wesson again, put on my coat and hat and got ready to leave. Whoever got to the subway first had the advantage. I wanted that to be me.

I'd promised to give Ed Killick a ring around nine . . . and it was nine o'clock now. I had nothing tangible for him except that Prager had taken the bait but that itself should be enough.

If I was guessing right, Theo Prager wouldn't be at the subway station, but a lookout man would be there. Somewhere on my way home I'd be jumped by Prager and one or two more of his friends. Whether I had the little souvenir he badly wanted or I was bluffing made no difference. He'd make sure I never returned home to set the law on him.

With Killick out of sight but not far behind I'd have an ace in the hole. One thing I relied on was that Prager believed I was willing to make a crooked deal . . . so I'd come alone. Everything depended on that — but everything.

The DA's number was busy. When I rang again it was still busy. At that hour of the night the regular staff would've quit and there'd be only one wire left open . . . which meant Ed was getting corns behind the ear listening to somebody's story of a long and trying life.

My watch said the time was five minutes after nine. I couldn't delay any longer or the whole deal would be off. My best bet would be to call Ed from the subway station when I'd shaken off the lookout. Then I could stick around until Killick showed up.

If he didn't, I'd have to play it off the cuff. I didn't fancy that, I didn't fancy it at all.

But time wasn't standing still. As I went out and pulled the door shut I told myself I'd have to rush if I wanted to stop off at a pay station and call Ed before I got to the subway. It would be safer to do that . . . a whole lot safer . . .

My thoughts froze about there. I'd used my left hand to close the door when I went out into the hallway so I was facing half-right when something prodded me in the back of the neck.

A thin voice said, "Open up again, smart guy, unless you want to get it right here. All one to me. This thing's got a silencer."

I didn't think he was kidding. I didn't think it was either the time or the place to do any sort of thinking. Right then I had as much use for ideas as I had for the hole in the head that was coming my way.

With the muzzle of the gun digging into my neck I unlocked the door and went inside. After that Prager stepped away from me. I didn't move a muscle. I'd met his kind.

With just a faint click the door closed. Prager said, "Put your hands on top of your head and make like a statue. If you act outa turn you'll get what Frankie got. It's as easy to frisk you lying down as standing up."

A man makes a logical statement, I don't argue. When I'd done as I'd been told he came close again, passed an arm round in front of me and removed the Smith and Wesson.

There were lots of things I could've done while he was doing it but I didn't reckon much of my chances. That's why I waited until he told me I could put my arms down.

" . . . Now face this way, nice and slow. That's right. We're gonna have a quiet chat, you and me. If I get what you say is mine I might give you a break . . . even if you don't deserve one."

He was wearing a dark topcoat, a dark pin-stripe suit and a black fedora. With his crisp white collar and sober necktie he could've passed for the vice-president of a bank.

They may have been the same clothes he'd worn for Frankie's going-away party. To me they looked the same. As an exercise in association that didn't make me feel too good.

His topcoat was unbuttoned. So was his jacket. Whoever had ironed his shirt didn't need to take lessons.

Sartorial elegance didn't make him any less of a liar. The cruel look in his predatory eyes told me what he intended to do when the time came.

I said, "What I don't deserve and what you'll give me will probably work out the same. But you better not do anything hasty. The thing you want isn't here."

"We'll see." He moved the gun lazily up and down. "If it's not here, you'll tell me where it is. Make no mistake about that — you'll tell me."

One thing I had to admit — he hadn't lied about the silencer. It made his long-barrelled Luger look even longer still. My guess was that the .22 he'd used to dispose of Connolly and Mike Tew had been buried somewhere in the brushwood or tossed into the lake.

Not that it mattered now. Nothing would get me out from behind the eight-ball unless he took his eyes off me for a second. It wasn't long but it would give me half a chance. I was prepared to settle for that.

The gun quit moving. In the same dead

voice, Prager said, "If you talk now, you could save yourself a load of grief. That's good advice, believe — "

It was the sudden noise of the phone bell that stopped him. With no expression on his tight-skinned face he stood looking at me, the Luger pointed in a straight line from his hand to my middle.

When the bell went on ringing, he asked, "Were you expecting someone to phone you at this time?"

I said, "No. I was just going out to keep a date at the subway station on Broadway and East — "

"Button your lip!" The ferocity of a wild beast flared in his eyes and I reckoned I had no chance of that half-chance. I could see the knuckles of his gun hand whiten.

Guess I was saved by the bell. It quit ringing.

Prager took a long breath and let it out again. His hand relaxed.

Then he asked, "Who do you think was calling you?"

I said, "How would I know? That thing's a telephone, not a television. If

270

you're all that curious you should've let me answer it."

"Be satisfied — " he spread his feet farther apart — "be satisfied that I've let you go on living. Take off your topcoat and your jacket."

Taking them off was better than having them taken off. I did as I'd been told, dropping them on the floor like he said.

"Now — " he gestured with the Luger — "put your hands on your head again and go over there and stand with your face to the wall. If you turn round until I say you should you'll get a slug some place where you'll be a long time a-dying."

With my back towards him I couldn't tell if he put the gun down before he began going through my pockets. Made no material difference. He could always have picked it up faster than I could've leapt across the six-seven feet separating us.

After a couple of minutes, he said, "There's nothing here that ties me in with Jeff Connolly or the shack out Reedsville way that you've been yapping about."

"You're only telling me what I've already told you," I said.

"Then where is it?"

"Nowhere. The whole thing was a gag to make you tip your hand."

"You don't say? I'm not the trusting type so we'll go look-see. Make with the feet into your bedroom."

He kept not too near, not too far, behind me. When we were inside he ordered me again to stand with my face to the wall while he stripped my bed, tossed everything out of the clothes closet and emptied the drawers of the dressing chest.

By the time he was through, my arms had begun to ache from lack of circulation. I had only myself to blame but that didn't help.

At last, he said, "Now the bathroom . . . "

We went through the same routine with the same result. Then he prodded me back into the living-room.

In his cold mean voice that sounded less than human, he said, "Turn round. I never like to blast a guy unless I can enjoy the look on his face when he knows he's going to get a hot shell in the guts."

With anybody else I'd have reckoned he was throwing a scare into me so I'd come clean. But not Theo Prager. He played rough. And he played for keeps.

When I was facing him, he said, "You can put your arms down. Now, for the last time, where is this souvenir you think could send me to the death house?"

"There's no such thing," I said. "I was just stringing you along. You didn't need to give my apartment a going over. You've already frisked the place once."

His eyes crawled down to my middle and back up to my my face again. He said, "You're talking through the top of your head. I've never been in this dump of yours before tonight."

"Well, someone made a search of both my apartment and my office."

"Maybe so. But it wasn't me. How would I know before tonight about this thing I'm supposed to have left at the fishing lodge?"

That was a tricky answer. I said, "Makes no odds anyway. What I told you on the phone was all a bluff. I don't know a darn thing that could put you on the spot."

His thin mouth became even thinner. He said, "That's just where you are, buster. If it's any consolation, I believe you. But you've talked yourself into trouble . . . and you won't talk yourself out of it. I can't afford to let you go around flapping a loose lip."

With his free hand he pushed his hat back like he wanted to let his head cool off. Then he added, "You should've known better than to try playing both ends against the middle. It's a sucker game."

I said, "Guess you're right. But that doesn't mean you got to rub me out just because I tried to make a fast buck."

The perforated black tube of the silencer rose a little until it wasn't much more than an unwinking eye. At that distance he couldn't miss. I hadn't a chance or a half-chance or any sort of chance.

But I couldn't stand there and let him gun me down like a duck with its wings clipped. What was to be would be. I'd dug a pit for myself and fallen into it. That didn't mean I had to make the job easy for him.

As I braced myself to take off, I said, "What good will it do you? I can't prove you bumped Connolly and Mike Tew and hid Jeff's body so it's look like he'd doublecrossed his partner and gone off with the gems. Noboby would listen to me."

Prager shook his head very deliberately from side to side. A light had come into his eyes that made me feel sick in the stomach.

He said, "Somebody might . . . if you beat their ears in long enough. You would, too. A kibitzer never knows when to lay off. And you're sure a three-stripe kibitzer."

One thing I'd discovered, for what it was worth. He wasn't in a hurry to pull the trigger. He was having himself too good a time. And while he went on listening and talking I'd go on living.

I said, "Knock me off and you'll never find that safe deposit key. Without it you can whistle for the half-million dollars that Frankie stashed away. I wouldn't call that smart . . . would you?"

His attention was split two ways. It showed in his eyes. They'd lost the look of cruelty that made him less than an animal. He didn't know what to do and if he should do it.

This was the moment I'd been waiting for. Chance or no chance, it was all he'd give me.

So I took a long breath while he was making up his mind. I made it real long because the odds were it would be the last I'd ever get.

Maybe Prager guessed I was about to take a gamble. A pinched look came into his face and he took one short step backward, his hand tightening round the Luger.

That was as far as he got. I didn't have time to do anything, either. Someone knocked on the door with a hard set of knuckles.

Prager didn't take his eyes off me. He rode the surprise as though he'd been expecting a caller.

The gun warned me to keep quiet. In

276

case that didn't register he put a finger to his lips.

There was another knock at the door. A man's voice called out, "Open up, Bowman! I know you're there. I can see your light's on."

By then I reckoned I had nothing to lose. Now Prager was on the spot. He looked like he didn't know whether to have a shave or a shampoo.

I said, "Guess we've got ourselves a new kind of Mexican standoff. It's your move."

Outside in the hallway, the same voice said, "I don't know what gives but I'm coming in. Get away from the door!"

It was Ed Killick's voice. I didn't know if Prager recognized it and I didn't care a damn. This was the one and only break that would come my way.

Something smashed into the lock like a hammer-blow and the door shook. For a fraction of a second Prager took his eyes off me. And a fraction was enough.

I ducked to one side, swivelled and hurled myself at his legs as another blow struck the lock. I was taking off head

277

tucked into my shoulders, when the door burst open.

In that same moment I saw Prager step out of the way the Luger swinging to point straight at me. In that same moment Ed Killick had come through the doorway in a headlong dive.

He rolled over as he hit the floor. Then there was an explosive bang followed by what seemed like an echo.

I couldn't feel any pain. I had no idea where the slug had caught me. It hadn't been in the head because I could still see and hear and think.

But thinking achieved very little and nothing now made any sound. The whole world had gone silent and still.

Ed Killick hadn't moved after he struck the floor full length and spun on to his side. Piager was looking down at me, the Luger still pointed in my direction, his cruel eyes narrowed as though in concentration.

After what seemed a long time I saw his hand grip the butt of the gun tightly. In that same moment I also saw a small hole in his shirt front four-five inches below the base of his throat. Around it grew a widening crimson stain.

Then blood bubbled out of his mouth and he let go of the Luger. It hit the carpet and bounced close beside where I lay as the vicious light in his eyes blinked out.

Very slowly his knees gave way. Like a dummy filled with straw he pitched forward on to his face.

12

THE law did what the law had to do. Then they carted away a lump of dead meat that had once been a two-legged animal called Theo Prager.

That let some fresh air into the place. It also gave Henderson and Ed Killick and me more room to move around.

When I offered to fix them a drink, Henderson said I ought to know he never used alcohol. Killick said thanks for the offer but he'd have to refuse because he was still on duty and it wouldn't look good if he smelled of liquor.

That left me. After I'd thought about it I opted out, too.

All the time, Henderson and Killick had acted like two dogs warily sizing each other up. The atmosphere wasn't exactly hostile but neither was it cordial. They talked through me as well as to me, using me as a kind of clearing house.

After he'd refused a drink, Henderson

asked, "Did Prager actually admit he'd done the double shooting at Reedsville?"

"As good as," I said.

"That isn't good enough. We'll need something more positive before we can close the file."

"The most positive thing would be Prager's confession . . . and I can't see you getting that."

"Cut the comedy. You know darn well what I mean. The killing of Frankie Siccola must've been tied up with what happened at the fishing lodge."

Ed Killick seemed content to listen. Mostly he just kept quiet, his eyes flitting from Henderson to me as we bounced the ball to and fro.

I said, "Why must it?"

"Because the detail who worked on that Shoemaker robbery were pretty sure the gopher mob would've needed three pairs of hands. Frankie never soiled his . . . so I'd reckon Theo Prager supplied the third pair."

"And?"

"It sticks out a mile. Either Frankie planned the double-cross or Prager

281

worked it out for himself. And his scheme went one stage further. It left him with the whole jackpot."

"You're saying Prager killed all three of them," I said.

Henderson took a matchstick from his pocket and put it between his teeth. He asked, "Why not? Who was better placed to know Siccola's plans and how to get round them?"

The sour old man in my head had one or two questions of his own. " . . . *Didn't I say Diane Russell was taking you for a ride? How long will you go on falling for the slick line a dame throws you just because she flutters her eyelashes?*"

Maybe the old man was right. What I couldn't see was how Diane was going to show a profit.

I said, "Up to here it figures. But the five hundred thousand and dollar question has still to be answered. Where are the proceeds of the robbery?"

With the matchstick bobbling in the corner of his hard mouth, Henderson looked at me like he was measuring my scalp. He said, "If I know that I wouldn't be standing here listening to your rhetorical questions. You want me to spell it out for you?"

"I'd like that," I said. "After all the exercise, I'll get a headache if I do too much thinking."

"You've — " for the first time he was including Ed Killick — "you've already thought of it. Frankie went to Duffie's Hotel that night to wait for Prager's arrival with the diamonds. Where they'd been planted since the robbery is immaterial. Siccola wasn't able to collect them himself. He had to lie low or he risked facing the grand jury."

"So Theo Prager was his errand boy," I said.

"Sure. Who else? He'd been in it right from the start. But Prager didn't arrive with a package of cut stones. Instead he walked into Frankie's room with a gun. Now Prager had half a million bucks to provide for his old age. Figures, doesn't it?"

If Diane hadn't hired me I'd have gone along with it all the way. But . . . It was one helluva big but.

283

I said, "Loosely, just loosely. A couple of things keep getting in the way."

"Let's hear them."

"Well, one is — why did Prager stick around town after Frankie's death? Why didn't he take off for faraway places where he could live the life of Riley?"

"It was too soon," Henderson said. "He couldn't be sure that either Homicide or the DA's office weren't keeping tabs on him. All he had to do was wait until the heat was off and he'd be in the clear."

"You got a point there," Killick said.

He glanced at me, turned to Henderson again and added, "I think I know the second thing that's worrying Bowman. Why would Prager use a .45 on Siccola? What was wrong with the .22 that disposed of Connolly and Tew?"

Henderson transferred the matchstick to the other corner of his mouth. He said, "You're a bit late — both of you. That's been worrying me ever since I walked in here. But my problem isn't quite the same as yours and Bowman's.

284

I've an idea why Prager switched from a .22."

I said, "Could be he didn't want Homicide to link Frankie's death with what had happened at the fishing lodge."

In a flat voice, Henderson said, "I managed to get that far myself without any help. But it didn't solve my problem. If Prager shot Frankie with a .45 and later made an attempt on your life with the same weapon . . . well?"

"Why did he come here tonight — " Ed gave me a troubled look — "with a Luger? The captain's right."

"Not altogether," I said. "He can't have it both ways. Either Prager killed all three of them — Connolly, Tew and Frankie — or he didn't. I believe he was responsible for the shooting at Reedsville but I'm not sold on the rest of it."

"Now we're back to square one," Henderson said.

He took the matchstick from his mouth, snapped it in half and dropped the bits in his pocket. Then he included Ed Killick and me in a dark scowl and

285

added, "You two have more brains than all the law enforcement officers put together. So think about it. I'm sure you'll come up with the answer."

When he got to the door he didn't tell me good night. He didn't even act like I was there.

But before he went out he nodded to Killick and said, "See you around . . . "

After he'd gone and I couldn't hear his footsteps in the hallway any more, Ed grinned at me and asked, "What's got into him? Is he always like that with you?"

"Most always," I said. "Do you wonder why I don't let you call him a pal of mine?"

"No . . . Guess it must rub you the wrong way."

"You can say that again."

I brought out a bottle of rye and two glasses. Killick said, "Thanks, I reckon I will. It's been a long day and tomorrow's nearly with us . . . "

So we had a little drink. When Ed refused another, I said, "What about that trade we were going to do? I've kept my side of the bargain. Now it's your turn."

"You mean about the shot that came through your window?"

"What else?"

"Well — " he picked up his glass, drained the last few drops and put it down again — "I've an idea the party outside wanted to miss."

"Sounds crazy to me," I said.

"Not if you add this and that together. As Captain Henderson would say, think about it."

"Where do I start?"

"With the sort of people who were involved with the late Frankie Siccola. That shot could've been fired with the intention of either scaring you off or spurring you on . . . but not to kill. All depends on the company you keep."

It was a thought. I didn't feel inclined to share my supplementary thoughts with a wisehead like Ed Killick so I just let it ride.

He buttoned his coat and walked to the door and stood there twiddling the knob as though trying to remember something.

287

Then he gave me a kind of old-fashioned look. He said, "Time I hit the hay. I've had enough action for one night."

I said, "I've had enough for a lifetime. And now we're alone I want to say thanks."

"For what?"

"You saved my life . . . or have you forgotten?"

"Oh, that? Think nothing of it."

"Maybe you don't but I do. I'm all I've got."

He nodded and smiled, his near-ugly face reflective. As he opened the door, he said, "Call it luck. Darn good job you couldn't get me at nine o'clock. I'd have been hanging around the subway station."

"While I was in conference with Theo Prager."

"Yeh. Pulled a real fast one, didn't he?"

"His big mistake was in not getting me to answer the phone," I said. "That call was from you, I suppose?"

"Sure. When I got no reply I guessed

something must be wrong."

Ed went outside and stood tugging at his puffy nose for a moment before he looked back and said, "I thought I'd be too late. Glad I wasn't. 'Night . . . "

★ ★ ★

After a lot of thinking I got some of the pieces sorted out. Herman Polk and Connie fitted in a kind of way even if they'd only told me half a story — the half they wanted me to know. Diane Russell seemed more like the unknown quantity.

While I was trying to decide what my next step should be I opened a window to get rid of the smell of burned powder. I put the light off before I went near the window . . . just to take no chances.

Maybe Ed was right. Maybe he was wrong. I didn't want to know the hard way. Neither did I want to disprove the old tag that lightning never strikes twice in the same place.

When I switched the light on again I inspected the scar on one of the table legs where the shell from Prager's gun had ricocheted. Henderson had taken possession of the battered slug as well as the Luger. I was left with a chip out of my table and the recollection of a helluva fright.

The more I thought about it the less inclination I had for sleep. So I fixed myself a cup of coffee to make sure I'd keep awake. Then I called Diane Russell.

She hadn't gone to bed. The first thing I noticed was that she sounded kind of nervous. The second thing was that she didn't seem at all surprised to get a call from me. That upset some of my ideas.

I told her it was about time we had a heart-to-heart. " . . . Recent developments make it necessary that I give you a progress report."

In a careful voice, she asked, "What developments? What's happened since you spoke with me this afternoon?"

"Quite a lot," I said. "In fact, plenty. That's why I want to fill you in."

"When?"

"Tonight . . . that's if you're not afraid the neighbours will talk."

Without any feeling, she said, "The hell with my neighbours. If you want to stop by I'll put on the coffee."

I needed her coffee like I needed a broken arm. But all the same I said, "Fine. I'm on my way."

★ ★ ★

The weather forecast hadn't exaggerated. It was a cold night. The frost had thickened since I got back from Reedsville and there was a shimmering halo round the moon.

On a night like that, people didn't loiter. I didn't spot any stake-out when I left my apartment block and nobody tailed me when I rode a cab to Diane's place on Sussex Street. That should've made me feel easier in mind but it didn't.

Her address was a rooming house. It might've been considered superior to many others but it was still a rooming house. I reckoned Diane would do better for herself when she collected the fifty-thousand-dollar reward for Shoemaker's diamonds . . . if she collected.

A flight of scrubbed stone steps led up from the street. In the lobby there was a double row of mail boxes, each with a name and number. Diane's box said she lived on the third floor.

Like everybody else I had to walk up. The place might've been clean, well-maintained and respectable but I'd have preferred the house on Riverside Drive — over-furnished or not. Something told me so would Diane.

The lighting was adequate but no more than that. There should've been two lights on the third floor: one of them had been switched off. I got the idea the landlord's motto was a penny saved is a penny earned.

Diane didn't keep me waiting outside in the hallway. Soon as I tapped lightly on her door it opened.

I couldn't have described what she was wearing but she looked real sharp. Without a coat and hat she seemed more approachable. I wondered if she knew it had registered.

She said, "Come on in."

Her warm brown eyes were faintly nervous but I reckoned the circumstances justified a touch of nerves. I liked her warm sweet smile when she asked me to take off my coat.

" . . . You won't get any benefit from it when you leave if you keep it on. Gone very cold tonight, hasn't it?"

If she wanted to swap idle talk until we got down to cases, it was all right with me. So I chipped in with the remark that it looked like winter had all but arrived.

By the time I got half-way I'd have said she'd quit listening. That was also all right with me.

Her living-room was furnished in the way I'd always liked — simple yet tasteful. It made me feel at home. So did she.

When I'd draped my coat over the back of a chair and sat down, she asked, "Could you use some coffee now . . . or would you prefer to wait a while?"

"I'll wait," I said.

"Well, whenever you're ready — " she perched herself on a chair facing mine, crossed her legs and studied me with wide inquiring eyes — "just tell me."

293

"I'll do that," I said. I wondered how she'd react when I told her what I was thinking.

Maybe it wasn't very gallant to carry a gun when calling on a lady but the hard lump of the Smith and Wesson pressing against my stomach did more for me than a bunch of flowers would've done for her. The events that had taken place since I'd first met pretty Diane had taught me that if I didn't look out for myself nobody else would.

While she went on looking at me she clasped her hands round one knee and leaned back so that the smooth lines of her throat showed to best advantage. It was the kind of mannerism Connie had . . . and not the only one. Both of them were on the make.

I'd had that sour feeling before — many times before. Money or no money, I wanted out.

Guess she sensed it. The warm light in her eyes cooled off and she lost her air of nervousness. Instead she looked worried. If I hadn't felt the way I felt I'd have felt a little bit sorry for her.

She said, "You're different somehow. What is it?"

"Life's getting kind of hectic," I said. "It's beginning to look as though neither of us will get any dividend out of this affair."

That worried her even more. She asked, "Why do you say that?"

"Because the one guy who may have known the inside story of Shoemaker's diamonds did something foolish to-night."

"What do you mean?"

"He went and dropped dead in my apartment," I said.

"How — " she moistened her lips — "how did it happen?"

"If you must know, he was on the losing end of a gun battle."

"I — I don't understand."

"It's not difficult. He intended to kill me but I got a lucky break. He didn't."

After a long brittle silence, Diane got up and began walking restlessly here and there. She picked things up and put them down and all the time she tried to avoid looking at me.

At last, she turned and said, "You're angry with me . . . I know. But you shouldn't really blame me for what's happened. I warned you right from the start that there was an element of risk."

"You sure did," I said. "In fact, you went farther than that. Your warning was that somebody might try to kill me. Well, somebody has — twice."

When she tucked in her lower lip and bit on it like she didn't quite know what to say, I added, "Tonight's attempt was for real."

Anger darkened her nice brown eyes. She swallowed, took a quick breath, and said, "None of this has been my fault. I'm sorry about it . . . but you went into the affair with your eyes open. You've no right to make me responsible."

I said, "Who says you're responsible? The only thing puzzling me is why you don't ask who it was that left my apartment in a basket."

Her anger vanished. Confusion took its place — not guilt. She looked like she thought I was being stupid.

All of which meant my suspicions had

been unjustified. I'd have gambled my life on it.

The old man inside me whined " . . . *Maybe that's just what you're doing.*"

Diane said, "I'll tell you why I never asked. If I won't be able to claim the reward from the insurance company, I don't give a damn who it was that got shot in your apartment. And while we're on the subject, I don't give a damn for you, either. Now get out and leave me alone."

Some women look even prettier when they get in a temper. Diane Russell was one of them. She could almost make me forget she'd been Frankie's bed-warmer.

I said, "Whoa . . . hold on there. What have I done?"

"If you'd seen the way — " there were tears in her eyes and I know real tears when I see them — "the way you've been looking at me you wouldn't have to ask."

"A guy doesn't deserve a bawling out just because of the way he looks," I said. "Now quit crying and let's talk this thing over like adults."

She wiped the back of her hand across her eyes and gave me the nearest thing to a scowl that would fit on her pretty face. She said, "You've got a gall if you think I'm shedding tears because you hurt my feelings. I'm mad at you — that's all — just plain mad. If you don't go away I'll scream."

Maybe she didn't mean it but it sounded real enough. So I stood up.

I said "OK. If that's how you want it, I'll go. But first we have a couple of details to discuss."

"Never mind the details." She glanced down at the smudge of mascara on her hand and scowled again. "Give me a handkerchief."

Guess I should've gone while the going was good. That handkerchief routine is most always the tacit offer of a truce. With her it would mean she'd come out on the winning side.

But I didn't go. When she'd wiped her eyes dry she made a clean fold in the handkerchief and dabbed her mouth.

Then she said, "I'll send this to the laundry and let you have it back."

Her voice was different, her manner was different. Anybody would've thought we were old friends.

I said, "For the price you've paid, I can afford to throw in a handkerchief. And talking about money — "

"Keep it. The risks you've taken, you're entitled to more than five hundred dollars."

"Risks were inclusive. If you're terminating my employment I'll have to refund part of the retainer."

Diane half-smiled at that. And even half a smile did things for her that other women would like done to them.

She said, "Don't be pompous. Did I say you were fired?"

"No . . . but I don't usually wait until I'm tossed down the stairs by the seat of my pants."

In a crisp voice, she asked, "Mind if we get back to something more important? Who was the man who tried to kill you tonight?"

"Your ex-husband's insurance policy," I said. "A moron called Theo Prager."

Once again she moistened her lips. She

was subdued but not surprised.

When she'd put her thoughts in order, she said, "I remember Theo. He never did anything unless he had a very good reason. What had you found out about him?"

"Nothing. But he thought I'd got hold of evidence that could send him to the chair."

"Evidence concerning Frankie?"

"Not in the way you mean. But it must have some kind of bearing on the affair at Duffie's Hotel. I bluffed Prager into admitting — or as good as admitting — that he'd been responsible for the death of both Tew and Connolly."

Her eyes widened. She asked, "How do you know Jeff Connolly's dead?"

"Because I found his body under the fishing lodge where Mike Tew was killed. It'll be in tomorrow's papers."

Diane repeated that trick of retiring within herself. For a long time she stood rolling the crumpled handkerchief into a ball while she stared through me and beyond me.

At last, she said, "So it wasn't Connolly

who did it. I should've guessed that long ago. Frankie used Prager to work a double-cross. And in the end Theo double-crossed his master."

She looked at me and shrugged. Then she added, "Now I understand why you told me neither of us would show a dividend."

I said, "Well, not exactly. I only suggested it was beginning to look that way."

"You mean — " she didn't sound very enthusiastic — "there's still a chance you can locate the letter of authority?"

"Sure. And I'll go on hunting for it. That's why you hired me, isn't it?"

"But if — " The rest of her thought hung like an invisible barrier between us.

There was no hurry, no need to force the issue. I could afford to wait. The five hundred dollar retainer would keep her in credit a while longer.

She took plenty of time to straighten out her ideas. Then she asked, "How will you ever find it now if it was Prager who killed Frankie?"

"If . . . " I said.

That seemed to add to her confusion. While she was chasing around to see where she'd gone wrong, I added, "Assuming he did, the letter is most likely to be some place where he laid his head nights. He wouldn't carry it around in his pocket."

"Probably not." She wasn't exactly bubbling over with expectation. "Do you know where he lived?"

"No . . . but neither does Homicide. It'll take them some time to trace his address."

"What good will that do us? Unless you get there before they do — "

"That's the whole point. I will."

"How? You just told me you don't know where he was living."

"But somebody else knows the address," I said. "Frankie's widow."

"You mean — " Diane stared at me with narrowed eyes — "you mean that dumb broad, Connie Munroe?"

"Well, her proper legal title is Mrs Connie Siccola — "

"Don't give me that stuff!"

302

"All right. Have it your own way. We'll stick to Connie and save argument. The main thing is I asked Connie to get a message to Prager for me this evening and she did. That's why he came to my apartment with the idea of getting rid of me."

Realization showed in Diane's face. She said, "I get it now. You didn't tell the police it was you who'd contacted Theo Prager."

"Correct. I let them think he phoned to warn me off . . . and I'd bluffed him into believing I had proof he'd shot Connolly and Tew."

"And with Theo dead — " she came a little nearer and looked up at me with her head tilted — "they'll never have reason to think any different."

"Correct again," I said.

"So you'll get his address from Connie and go there and search the place until you find that letter of authority . . . m-m-m?"

"If it's there to find," I said.

She cupped her face in her hands and became all thoughtful. She said,

303

"Don't say things like that. It's got to be there. I'm only afraid Connie might tell Homicide the address. They're bound to question her."

"Why?"

"Because Theo must've visited Frankie's house very often in the past eighteen months. She couldn't have avoided knowing where he lived."

"That goes for you, too," I said. "You were married to Frankie all of four years and Prager was his bodyguard during that time."

Diane just went on looking up at me. Without a flutter of her smudged eyelashes, she said, "If I ever did know the address, I've forgotten it. But Connie's so dumb she'll tell them soon's they ask."

"Well, she's no reason to keep it a secret. But, all the same, she won't talk. She's scared of dealing with the law."

In a casual voice, Diane asked, "What makes you think she'll talk to you?"

"Because she isn't scared of me. I got her to pass on a message to Theo Prager without any argument."

"That shows you just how dumb she is."

It was only a remark but something about it irked me. I said, "Maybe it's a tribute to my powers of persuasion."

Diane took her hands from her face and gave me a slow smile that didn't mean she thought I was a wit. I began to get some more of the ideas I'd had the day they planted Frankie in Belleview Cemetery.

Very gently, she asked, "What would you do if I offered you half the fifty-thousand-dollar reward?"

I wasn't sure where that sort of question would lead me but I didn't want to go there. So I said, "There might be no reward. I believe in the old saying you should first hatch your chicken."

"Skip the old sayings." Her nice brown eyes honestly wanted to know. "What would you do if I offered you half?"

"Take it," I said.

Her smile changed to soft laughter. I liked her when she laughed like that. It made me feel good.

She asked, "What would you do when it was yours?"

"Spend it," I said.

"All on yourself?"

That way led to the road of no return. Like I'd told myself once before, it might be fun. The only trouble was it might work out a pretty steep price.

I said, "What's wrong with having myself a good time?"

All of a sudden she quit smiling. With the light of a distant promise in her eyes, she said, "Nothing. But two can always make a good time twice as good."

Then she moistened her lips. In a shaky voice, she said, "You can't be so stupid that you don't know what I'm trying to say. Guess I must be so darn ugly you can't bear to come near me."

There was only one step separating us. I took that step. Now we were so close I could see my twin reflections in her eyes.

I said, "See how wrong you are? Here I am. Can't get much nearer, can I?"

"Oh yes, you can."

She put her arms round my neck and

306

pressed herself against me. In a shaky voice, she said, "I'm not just offering a fifty per cent share of the money. You get me, too."

Her hands were cool, her lips like ice. I tried to remember what she'd been to Frankie Siccola but it didn't protect me. To resist the demands of her body was asking too much.

The sour old man began saying over and over again " . . . *Henderson was right. He said times must be grim if you have to make a play for Siccola's cast-off. Henderson was right . . . Henderson was right . . .* "

She began to tremble and her mouth became sweet fire. I persuaded myself that this was merely an interlude, the satisfaction of a hunger shared by two people who broke no law, owed no loyalty to anyone. I wasn't despoiling the pure in mind or in body. For four years she'd given Frankie Siccola his fun. He'd possessed her more times than she could count.

Frankie had taken. I was accepting what she freely offered. That was the

307

difference between Frankie and me. There had to be a difference. There just had to be.

Diane unfastened the neck of her dress and wriggled free to take hold of my hand. When I stroked the smooth nakedness of her throat and shoulder she caught her breath and gripped me fiercely.

Now the road back was impassable. Yet I couldn't go on. I was trapped between desire and revulsion.

Like the re-play of a movie we were once again in Belleview Cemetery. She'd gone a few paces along the paved walk and I was standing beside the grave of Frankie Siccola.

She was saying " . . . *He treated me like a dog and yet, while he lived, there was only one guy in the world for me . . . If he'd got rid of that blonde tramp I'd have gone back to him . . .* "

And the old voice in my head wouldn't leave me alone. " *. . . if he were alive she'd be with him now. She'd be going to bed with him, not you. Frankie would be pawing her, not you. It's Frankie she wants, not you. It's Frankie she's* *giving herself to. You're a stand-in for a sonovabitch like Frankie Siccola. From here on in if you can face yourself in the shaving mirror you're lower than he was . . . "*

The honey of her lips changed to vinegar. While she still clung to me, I said, "A partnership's got to be all or nothing. Won't work if we have any secrets from each other."

Against my mouth, she asked, "What do you mean?"

"I have to know everything about that night at Duffie's Hotel. Was it you who put a .45 bullet in Frankie's head?"

She dug her nails into the back of my neck like a cat flexing its claws. It wasn't meant to hurt.

When she'd closed her teeth on my lower lip in a playful bite that didn't hurt, either, she said, "I've been wondering if you'd ask me that."

"OK. So now I've asked you. What's the answer?"

Without letting go of me, she said, "You must be crazy."

"Why? D'you expect me to believe you

aren't capable of doing it?"

"That's beside the point. Why should I hire you to locate Frankie's killer if I'd done it myself? I wouldn't need you. I'd already have both the key and the letter of authority."

I said, "Not if somebody got to the hotel before you did, slugged Frankie and took the letter off him. The party who did the slugging probably frisked his room but never thought of examining the little bible in his piece of baggage."

Diane leaned back and looked at me in open surprise. She said, "But it wasn't in Frankie's grip. He sent it to me. I told you that."

"So you did. But it isn't necessarily true. Could be you learned he was stopping at Duffie's Hotel and you paid him an unexpected visit."

She went on looking at me while her fingertips titillated the back of my neck. In a taunting voice, she said, "A partnership's no good unless it's based on mutual trust. Ours won't get off the ground if you suspect I'm a liar."

"All right, convince me I'm wrong. Did

Frankie send you the bible with the key inside it?"

"Yes . . . and that's the solemn truth."

It sounded true. But everything and everybody that had ever been connected with Frankie were all so tainted with his rotten crookedness that I couldn't trust my own best instincts.

I let it ride for the time being. I said, "One thing more before we blow out the candle and go to bed. It won't be much fun for me if I'm scared to fall asleep in case I wake up with my throat cut."

Diane shook her head impatiently. She said, "Any more of this and you can go home to your own bed. I'm rapidly losing the inclination."

Maybe it was her tone, maybe the look in her nice brown eyes, that made me feel all the excitement had been on my side. Her promise of half the fifty thousand had no permanent worth. Promises could be broken. As a down payment, the offer of herself wasn't much of a collateral.

I said, "I'm sorry about that but I don't aim to finish up like Frankie. I've got to be sure."

"About what?"

"Something you might call loyalty. We're people — not a couple of dogs in the street."

"So?" She put both hands on my shoulders, pushed herself farther away and stood looking at me without emotion, her hair dishevelled, her dress gaping open almost to the waist.

"In some things, we're two of a kind," I said. "But I don't betray somebody's trust."

"Meaning that I do."

"Well, I think you did. Not that I blame you after the way you were treated by Siccola."

"Blame me for what?"

"Squealing on Frankie to the DA's office. It was you, wasn't it?"

"No." She used one hand to close the front of her dress as she drew back another step. "How could I have squealed on him? He never told me anything the law could use to make trouble."

"He told you about the stolen gems," I said.

"That was different. He only turned to

312

me because he was desperate. When the chips were down he realized he couldn't trust anyone but me."

If she'd left it there I'd have been convinced. But being what she was, she added, "I wouldn't have let him down. I'd have stood by him. He was more important to me than the diamonds."

"After he'd threatened you with a faceful of acid if you didn't provide him with grounds for divorce? Don't make me laugh! Your only concern was what was in it for you."

Her simmering anger boiled over. She said, "That's a lie! It was for his sake that I risked going to the hotel and — "

The breath caught in her throat. Suddenly she wasn't pretty any more. Suddenly I knew what people meant when they said truth could be ugly. It was the truth I saw in her face.

She didn't say a word, she didn't move, as I walked over to the phone. Guess it was just as well. Whatever she'd tried to say wouldn't have prevented me from doing what had to be done.

Before I could pick up the receiver the

bell rang. Must've given her as big a shock as it gave me. She went very pale and a hunted look came into her eyes.

In a husky voice, she said, "Don't take that call. I've got to talk with you. I've got to make you believe I didn't kill Frankie. He was dead when I got there . . . "

The bell went on ringing. One half of me listened to it, the other half watched Diane Russell break into little pieces.

" . . . He'd asked me to pick up the letter of authority. When I'd collected the diamonds I was to make a reservation for two on the next plane to Miami and then come back to the hotel for him . . . "

The bell was still ringing. She didn't seem to hear it as the words poured out as though they'd been pent up too long.

" . . . Like he'd arranged, the door wasn't locked so I just walked right in . . . and I found him lying there dead. That's the gospel truth."

I said, "Did you make reservation for two on that plane or just one ticket for yourself?"

It nearly choked her but she managed to say, "Just one. You can see I'm being honest with you or I wouldn't — "

"You meant to kill him when he handed you the letter of authority. Is that what you're saying?"

"Yes, yes! I hated him for what he'd done to me and I despised him for the way he'd come crawling when he was in trouble, the way he'd taken me for granted. Sure, I'd have killed him! Isn't that enough to convince you I'm telling the truth?"

It cost her nothing to admit what I'd already guessed for myself. Confession of intent was better than admission of murder.

I said, "Don't bother to convince me. Save your breath for the judge and jury."

By then the bell was drilling holes in my skull. So I picked up the receiver.

Before I had time to say anything, the party at the other end asked, "Is Miss Diane Russell there?"

It sounded like a voice I'd heard before but the telephone does tricks with people's voices. I said, "Yes, she is. Who wants her?"

"Maybe the butcher, the baker or the candlestick maker. For my part they can have her. It's you I want."

His voice was familiar and not a trick of the phone. I said, "How did you know I was here?"

Herman Polk thought that was funny enough to rate a laugh. He said, "I got a crystal ball."

"Don't play damnfool games or I'll hang up on you. How did you know?"

"When I rang your own place and got no reply I made a list of likely numbers and tried this one first."

"Why here?"

"Where else would you go to discuss the sudden death of a guy called Theo Prager?"

Diane was trying to listen-in. By the look on her anxious face all she could hear was my end of the conversation.

"Proves that another old saying is wrong," I said. "It's not only bad news that travels fast."

"Don't think I'm crying my eyes out," Polk said.

"How did you get to know?"

"Like I told you, I hear things. Some of the more interesting ones I picked up from Prager. He wanted a well-paid job when poor Frankie died and so he chipped in with a lot of useful information . . . such as his part in a certain double-cross."

I said, "So all your talk was a load of malarkey. It's a parcel of cut stones you're after."

That shook Diane. As she fastened up the front of her dress she seemed to have trouble with the zip.

Polk gave a rumbling laugh. He said, "Half a million bucks is a lot of gravy. Exchange rate is good, too. There'd be enough to split several ways."

"With you getting the thick end of the take . . . of course."

"But of course."

"So when Prager frisked my flatlet and my office and didn't find what he was looking for you dangled a thousand dollar carrot under my nose."

"Prager didn't tell me he'd done any frisking," Polk said. "I don't ask for running commentaries. I'm only interested in results."

I said, "To get results you turned an animal loose on Pamela Connolly."

"That's something I wouldn't know, either."

"You know damn' well he scared her to death . . . and that's no figure of speech."

Diane had a numb look on her face. She seemed to be in the grip of an emotion greater than fear.

The phone said, "If Prager did that he was stupid. You don't get information out of somebody who's dead."

"He didn't understand that because he was a moron. When he called on me this evening all he wanted was to save his own skin."

"If you crowd a guy like Prager you can't blame me for what happens," Polk said.

"The law might take a different view."

"You must be joking! Who's to prove that Prager was working for me? The law can't make the dead testify."

I said, "You've already made that point. I'm more interested in me.

If Prager told you I'd been hired to investigate the shooting of Frankie Siccola, somebody must've told him. Who?"

Diane moved stiffly. I saw her look towards a table with two narrow drawers and some books standing on top. Beside the books there was one of those cylindrical gilt calendar things that can have month, day and date varied by turning knobs at each end.

When she saw me watching her she glanced down at the floor and began playing with her hands. From then on I kept my eyes on her.

Polk said, "A dumb broad told him — Frankie's grieving widow. Guess she didn't think there was any harm in telling the guy who'd been her late husband's strong-arm man."

"This is where I came in," I said. "You didn't call me just to have a gabfest. What do you want?"

"What I've paid for — your services. But now you know my interest is purely a financial one."

"Too bad. You've backed the wrong

horse. Those diamonds aren't mine to give away."

"Better change your mind," Polk said. "My ponies never lose. This gee's got a thousand bucks on the nose."

"You can have your money back."

"Uh-uh. Once you took it, it's yours. Remember saying something about being in my pocket? Well, you can't climb out."

He sounded tough. He also sounded like he meant it. I knew Herman Polk didn't talk for the sake of hearing his own voice.

While I was adding up the score I caught sight if Diane edging towards the table with the books and the cylindrical calendar standing on it. That made twice.

I reckoned she knew what day it was and I didn't think she had a yen to curl up with a good book. So I was left with better than an idea there was something in one of the drawers that she'd like to get her hands on.

At that I brought out the Smith and Wesson and showed it to her. It seemed to curb her wanderlust. She quit sidling towards the little table against the wall and turned her head away so I wouldn't see the look in the eyes.

Then I asked Polk, "You threatening me?"

"Don't be a damn fool. We need each other. Is Diane Russell there?"

"Yes."

"Well, when I've spelled out my proposition, you can put it to her. How much is she paying you?"

"Enough." I thought of those moments when she'd filled me with the old madness and I added, "More than enough."

Herman Polk wasn't slow. He laughed one of his rumbling laughs and said, "I was talking about money. In terms of hard cash I'll give you double."

"To renege on a client?"

"No. Whatever she expects to get out of it she'll get the same from me. There's plenty for all in this deal."

He was a cheat and a liar. Polk followed the tradition of Frankie Siccola. Their kind never parted with a dime unless they had to. And Herman Polk didn't have to. If I were crazy enough

321

to fall for his proposition I'd go the same way as Connolly and Tew.

I said, "That's where you're backing the wrong horse again. There's only the reward from the insurance company . . . and you haven't a Chinaman's chance of getting a slice of that."

"If you back the odds — " his voice hadn't changed "you'll be good and sorry. I promise you."

"All right, now you've had your say. So listen to this. I don't intend to — "

"The day I listen to a two-bit shamus, that'll be the day."

"I don't intend to be a party to any deal involving stolen property," I said. "If I locate Shoemaker's diamonds they go back where they belong . . . and you can go to hell where you belong."

There I hung up. While Diane watched me with frightened eyes, I dialled Ed Killick's home number.

13

H E took long enough to answer. I knew where he'd said he was going when he left me so I gave him plenty of time. Some people take a lot of rousing after a hectic night.

At last the bell quit ringing at the other end. Ed asked, "Yes? Who is that?" He sounded only half-awake.

I said, "You must be on sleeping pills. If there was a fire you'd be like Sunday's dinner."

"Oh, it's you."

He cleared his throat a couple of times. Then he said, "I was darn tired and I came straight home to bed. That's where you should be. What's the idea of waking me at this hour?"

"There's something I've got to discuss with you."

"Won't it keep till morning? Nothing we can do right now and I'm as dopey as — "

"It won't keep," I said. "Slap some cold water on your face and get out of here as soon as you can."

"Out where? I'm in bed even if you're not . . . and that's were I'm going to stop. The most I'm prepared to do is listen . . . so let's hear what's on your mind."

I said, "Don't be pig-headed. This is important."

"It would have to be a national emergency to get me out of bed on a freezing cold night after a long hard day's scratching around on the Siccola affair."

"That's the whole point. You may not need to do any more scratching around. Remember what you said Monday night?"

"Monday?" The phone clattered as though he'd dropped the receiver and picked it up again. "That was the day of Frankie's funeral. More than a few remarks have been passed since then. Which one are you talking about?"

"You said you'd like to nail the party who did the killing. He'd make a good replacement for Frankie."

Diane seemed to be crushed under the weight of her fear. If I hadn't known what she'd planned for me right from the start I could've felt some compassion for her.

Ed Killick said, "Don't remember those exact words — but the sentiment's OK. What's all this in aid of?"

"Just a matter of sex — the wrong sex. If you'd like to meet her she's all yours."

"If I'd like?" Now he was sharp and wide awake. "Where is she?"

"A rooming house on Sussex Street — third floor."

"But that's the address of Siccola's ex-wife. You sure you know what you're doing?"

"Quite sure." Diane was looking at me like she'd seen a ghost. "She's already admitted she went to Duffie's Hotel that night. Shouldn't be too difficult for you and Henderson to prove she killed Frankie Siccola."

"He deserved what he got — and more. Pity a woman has to take the rap for sweeping up a piece of garbage. Have you spoken with Henderson yet?"

"No. I thought I'd wait until you'd heard her story yourself."

"Yeh. Tough break whichever way you look at it. I was hoping it would turn out to have been Prager after all."

"Are you — " it was crazy but I had to ask — "are you trying to say we should forget the whole thing now Prager's very conveniently dead?"

In a gruff voice, Ed Killick said, "Be your age. I never let my private feelings interfere with my official duty. "See you soon . . . "

* * *

The next half-hour was a long time. Diane sat with her face in her hands, now and again peeking up at me through her fingers, mostly remaining still and silent.

I knew she was bound to make one more attempt to put pressure on me before Ed arrived and I was right. At the end of fifteen minutes she began making little whimpering noises that grew louder when I ignored them.

Then she raised her head and looked at me with tears in her eyes. She said, "I didn't kill Frankie. You've got to believe that."

"Don't tell me," I said. "Tell it to the judge."

"They can't arrest me. There isn't a scrap of evidence. I'll deny everything you say I told you. It'll be your word against mine."

"That's Homicide's worry. They get paid for it."

"You're a fool."

She brooded for a while. Then she tried again.

This time she used a different technique. She asked, "Was it so very wrong of me to make you think I only wanted the reward offered by the insurance company?"

"Receiving stolen property is as bad, if not worse, than the original theft," I said. "But I don't give a damn for the legal position. When I trust somebody I don't like to be told a pack of lies . . . and you lied to me all along the line."

"Suppose I were to tell you the truth now — the whole truth?"

327

Her nice brown eyes were still wet with tears. She sounded plaintive and she looked honest.

"Nobody's stopping you," I said.

"Well, for a start — " she moistened her lips, felt behind her for my handkerchief and dabbed her eyes — "Frankie didn't send me the key. I was to collect it along with the letter of authority."

"When you went to Duffie's Hotel?"

"Yes. That was what we arranged on the phone."

"He told you then what it was all about?"

"Yes."

"What did you intend to do after he'd given you the letter and the safe-deposit key?"

"I — I don't know. After hating him for months I was tempted . . . "

"To pay him back for all he'd done to you," I said.

"Yes."

"But you didn't get the chance because he was dead when you got there?"

"That's right." Her manner brightened. "Maybe I would've killed him. I can't say now what I'd have done. I'm all confused."

"Did you have a gun with you?"

She hesitated just too long before she said, "Yes . . . but I didn't use it."

"If you're all confused, how do you know? Because Frankie was lying on the floor doesn't mean he was dead. He'd been slugged and robbed of the letter. I can guess that for myself. You made sure he wouldn't wake up while you were searching his grip. That's how you got hold of the pocket bible, isn't it?"

"No. I went through his things and I found where he'd hidden the key but I didn't kill him. What must I do to convince you?"

She got up and came towards me and took hold of the fronts of my coat. With a tremor in her voice, she said, "I don't know who you were talking with on the phone but you could tell him you'd made a mistake. He'd believe you, wouldn't he?"

I said, "Guess he might, at that. Like most guys who are tough he's got a sentimental streak."

"Well, then . . . " She cupped my face in her hands and offered me her mouth in token surrender. "If he thinks I deserve a break after all that Frankie did to me, why must you destroy everything you and I could share together? With half a million dollars we could go to wonderful places and forget Prager and Herman Polk and Frankie and — "

"Sounds real romantic," I said. "But that kind of romance I can do without. It's got no future."

"What — " she didn't need to ask but it would've looked bad if she hadn't — "what do you mean?"

I said, "If and when we got our hands on those diamonds, I could kiss this life goodbye. You'd give me the same as Connolly and Tew and Theo Prager — a slug between the ears."

"No . . . no, you're wrong. Half of it will be yours. We'll go away together and there's nothing I won't do to make you happy . . . "

The lie showed in her eyes and on her lips. She'd done her best but she couldn't hide it from me.

In the midst of her frantic protests I caught hold of her by the arms and flung her away. She stumbled and almost fell and then collapsed into her chair.

As she pushed herself upright she was panting with fury. She said, "All right, now you'll get nothing! D'you hear — nothing! You can forget the five grand I promised you and everything else. You fool, you gawdamned fool! Did you really think I'd pay you a quarter of million dollars for the pleasure of your company in bed?"

I said, "Guess not. Looks like this is the end of a beautiful friendship."

She called me something she must've picked up from a stevedore. So I added, "Pity you won't come into any of that money. You could've bought yourself a cake of soap to wash out your mouth."

At that she laughed. It wasn't a very pleasant laugh.

She said, "Those diamonds are as good as mine. If Theo Prager had the letter of authority I know where he'll have hidden it . . . but no one else does. Soon as this affair's all over . . . " She laughed again.

"You're overlooking one thing," I said. "I happen to have the safe-deposit key."

Diane thought that was real funny. She shook her head at me and said, "You must be a bigger dope than I imagined. Do you think I'd hand over the genuine key to a guy I'd never seen before the day Frankie was burried?"

She may have lied to me all along the line but I knew this time she was telling the truth. I didn't need any convincing. It figured.

So she was entitled to call me a dope. When I'd monkeyed with that little pocket bible I'd merely been replacing her substitute with my substitute. What riled me most was that I'd risked getting a hole in the head for the sake of a phoney key taped under the drawer of my desk.

Even if there'd been anything worth saying I wouldn't have said it. Talk would get me nowhere. I'd been cut down to size . . . period.

It was close on half an hour since I'd spoken with Ed. He was due any time now. I reckoned my best bet was to leave the rest of the action to the DA's special investigator. He'd know the right things to do. For my part the sooner the better.

While we waited, I kept an eye on Diane and she kept an eye on me. It wasn't a long wait. He arrived as near as made no difference thirty minutes after I'd given him the news that might get him a rise.

I heard a car roll up and stop outside the rooming house. The motor died . . . a car door slammed shut without too much noise . . . a pair of shoes trotted up the steps from the sidewalk.

About then I got to thinking about Herman Polk. He'd had plenty of time to do some thinking about me. If he'd sent a gorilla by the name of Carl . . .

It didn't sound like I imagined Carl's footsteps would sound but I was no expert on footsteps. So I kept a hand within easy reach of the .38 while I listened to the same pair of feet coming up the stairs and along the hallway.

They halted outside the door. Someone knocked two-three times.

I said, "Who is that?"

"Killick. Who did you think it was — the butler?"

Judging by his voice he wasn't in an amiable mood. I got the idea he didn't enjoy being roused out of a warm bed on a cold night.

When I let him in he gave Diane a long hard look while he fingered the indentation in his chin. He didn't seem to fancy what he saw.

The way she looked back at him made me feel she wasn't scared any more. It was almost as though his rugged face wasn't as forbidding as she'd feared. I got the idea she thought she could handle him better than she'd handled me.

Yet there was also something in her eyes I couldn't understand — a faint look of what might've been doubt. That was as near as I could get.

By then Ed had come close to me and asked in a low voice, "Have you got anything from her in writing?"

"No, I reckoned I'd better leave that to you."

"Why me? I've been thinking about it

on the way here and I'd say this is a job for Homicide."

"Frankie Siccola was your baby," I said. "Don't you want to be in at the finish?"

"If it is the finish. What she admitted to you isn't real evidence."

Killick turned his back on me and walked into the middle of the room and studied Diane with his head thrust forward. He asked, "Do you know who I am?"

"No." What I'd thought was a look of doubt in her eyes had gone. Now she was just mildly puzzled.

It tinged her voice as she added, "So you can't make anything out of it. I've never seen you before."

"Well, I've seen you. I was at Frankie Siccola's funeral Monday morning. Maybe you didn't notice me because you had other things on your mind."

"Better things is how I'd put it."

What she was saying wasn't what she was thinking. I wondered if she still had her mind on the little table with its stack of books and the cylindrical gilt calendar.

335

Ed stroked his puffy nose between finger and thumb. Then he said, "My name's Killick. I'm a special investigator for the District Attorney's office concerned with the homicide of your ex-husband, Frank Siccola. From what Mr Bowman has told me you have admitted — "

"I've admitted nothing," Diane said. "Your pal, Mister Bowman, is a damned liar."

"You deny all responsibility for the death of Siccola?"

"Sure I deny it! I haven't seen Frankie in months."

"He didn't communicate with you Tuesday or Wednesday of last week?"

"No."

She hadn't taken her eyes off Ed's face. For all the notice she took of me I might not have been there.

With a nod that could've meant anything, Ed Killick asked, "Have you ever been in Duffie's Hotel, the place where your ex-husband was found shot to death?"

Almost before she'd heard the whole question, Diane said, "No."

"So, if anybody says you were seen coming out of Siccola's room, that person is mistaken?"

"Not mistaken." Her mouth widened in a smile that didn't reach her eyes. "Non-existent. You can quit trying to kid me, mister. There's no such person."

Killick's near-ugly face didn't react one way or the other. He said, "That's where you could be making a mistake . . . but we'll let it lie at this time."

In the same placid voice, he asked, "Why did you hire Bowman?"

Diane flicked a glance at me. She said, "I wanted him to locate Frankie's killer."

"Yes, I know what you wanted. The question is why. Do you expect me to believe you were prepared to spend good money to avenge Siccola's death?"

"You can believe it or not. Cuts no ice with me. For my part you and Bowman can go drop dead."

"That I can believe. Why did you think he might be more successful than the Homicide Bureau?"

"Well, he couldn't be less successful.

They were getting nowhere in a long time. I thought it was worth speculating a few dollars."

Without looking at me, she added, "Now if you called that a mistake I'd agree with you."

Ed nodded again. He asked, "How much is a few dollars?"

"If you're all that curious you can ask Bowman. He's right behind you."

"I'm asking you. Miss Russell. Any reason why you shouldn't answer?"

"None at all. I paid him a retainer of five hundred dollars."

"To describe a sum of that size as a few dollars you must be better fixed than your surroundings would indicate."

"Don't judge by my surroundings. How I choose to live is no damn' business of yours."

Killick said, "Don't get excited. I'm not interested in your way of life. What does concern me is the matter of finance. How was this sum of five hundred dollars made up?"

She didn't throw the answer at him this time. When her eyes had taken him to pieces, she said, "I don't see what difference it makes."

That was where Ed's manner suddenly changed. He said, "In that case, you won't mind telling me. If you refuse, I'll hand you over to Captain Henderson. He has a nice quiet room down at police headquarters for people who withhold information."

Diane lost some of her poise. She said, "You won't talk like that after I've spoken with my lawyer."

"Maybe not." Ed glanced at me with a veiled warning in his eyes. "Has Miss Russell called anybody while you've been here?"

I said, "No . . . and I think you're wasting time. Two-three hours in the sweatbox and she'll cough out enough answers to fill a book. Must have a good reason for not wanting to say how she paid me that retainer."

In a ragged voice, Diane said. "You keep out of this! I'm not afraid to say I gave you five one-hundred-dollar bills. But I still don't see what all the fuss is about."

"You will," Killick said. "When I've asked my next question, you will. Where did you get the five bills?"

That puzzled look put little lines at the corners of her eyes. If she was scared it didn't show.

But again she took her time before she said cautiously, "From the bank . . . I guess. Where else do you get money?"

"Which bank?"

"I — " now she was more scared than puzzled — "I don't have to answer that unless you tell me why you want to know."

"You're in no position to make your own terms, Miss Russell, but I'll tell you all the same." He pointed a long forefinger at her. "The hundred-dollar bills you gave Bowman have been checked . . . and they bear the serial numbers of bills issued by the Eastern Fidelity Bank of New York to a depositor who closed his account eight days ago."

Her face seemed to shrink. One hand crept inside the other as though seeking a place to hide when Killick added,

"The name of that depositor was Frank Siccola."

She swallowed, cleared her throat and swallowed again. Then she said drily, "I don't believe you. It isn't true."

He looked at me over his shoulder. I knew what he wanted. The veiled warning that had been in his eyes didn't need any explanation now.

A black lie doesn't change its colour when it's white-washed. Underneath it's still black.

The retainer she'd paid me was still in my pocket where it had been ever since Monday afternoon. Herman Polk's thousand dollars kept it company. Nobody had checked the serial numbers. I knew that. And Killick knew that I knew it.

But if he wanted me to play ball I could do no less. It was his one lie against all the lies that Diane had told.

So I shot her down with his ammunition. I said, "It's true all right. Eastern Fidelity say the hundred-dollar bills were issued to Siccola. The question is how you came into possession of them."

341

She held on to her captive hand and stood breathing little shallow breaths while Killick and I watched her wage an internal struggle. I knew she would find only one possible road of escape.

At last, she said, "OK. You win. I did get those hundred-dollar bills from Frankie . . . but not the way you think I got them. He gave me the money."

Ed drew back. His face told me what was in his mind.

He asked, "How?"

"By special delivery. I was to make a reservation for both of us on the plane to Miami."

"And did you?"

"No." With an effort, she added, "I couldn't."

"Why not?"

"Because I was too scared. I knew if I collected what Frankie wanted he'd have no further use for me."

"What had he asked you to collect?"

Diane shrugged. In a lifeless voice, she said, "The Shoemaker diamonds."

Ed took a long satisfied breath. Now he was acting like I wasn't there.

342

He said, "You're doing fine, Miss Russell, just fine. You help me and I'll help you. Where had he planted the diamonds?"

"In a safe-deposit. Along with the money for the plane tickets Frankie sent me the key."

"So — " Ed gave me another warning glance — "you went to the safe-deposit, collected half a million dollars worth of cut stones and — "

"No, I didn't. I couldn't get them without the letter of authority."

" — and then visited Duffie's Hotel where you put a bullet in Frankie's head because you had no further use for him. That's really what happened, isn't it?"

With a frantic look in her eyes, Diane said, "No, it isn't true! I didn't kill Frankie and I've never even seen the diamonds. You've got to believe me!"

Killick said, "In a pig's eye. All this is a load of apple-juice. Frankie didn't send you the key. After you'd killed him you searched his hotel room and you found it there. Why don't you come clean and save yourself a lot of trouble?"

343

"But I didn't kill him . . . I tell you I didn't."

Then her resistance finally crumbled. She put both hands over her face and began rocking from side to side.

"Now for the truth," Killick said. "Let's have the truth once and for all."

She looked up at him. In little more than a whisper, she said, "You'll have the truth. Frankie did send me the money by special delivery. And he also sent me the safe-deposit key. You can ask Bowman. I gave it to him."

Ed Killick didn't bother to look at me. As though in preparation for something that had to be just right, he took off his hat, scratched his ginger crewcut and put his hat on again. It was all done very deliberately.

In the same deliberate manner he went a step towards her. In a deliberate voice, he said, "I've had a bellyful of your lies. When you walked into Frankie's room you were carrying a gun. To get what you wanted you had to get rid of him. That was your intention all along, wasn't it?"

"Yes." Her hands dropped and she

made a face like she was in pain. "But I didn't kill him. He was dead before I got there. Nothing you can do will ever make me say I shot him."

"Eventually you will," Killick said. "Let's take it in easy stages. First of all you searched Frankie and helped yourself to the considerable sum of money he had in his pocket. Then you searched his grip. That was where you found the little bible in which . . . "

Ed seemed to lose the thread of what he was saying. I'd have said the look on Diane's face had knocked him off-course.

She was staring at him like he'd suddenly sprouted horns and a tail. That was how I felt, too.

In the time that had elapsed between one word and the next, my world of solid reality had fallen apart. Out of the pieces a new design was taking shape. For Ed Killick and me nothing would ever be the same again.

I could see his profile. It had set as though made of stone. That resolved my ultimate doubt. I now knew all the answers.

345

Very slowly and very carefully I felt inside my coat and wrapped my hand round the butt of the Smith and Wesson. Ed hadn't moved.

Diane moistened her lips, took an uneven breath and backed away from him until she bumped into the small table with its stack of books and gilt calendar. Her eyes were filled with the light of startled realization.

After a couple of attempts, she said, "I thought there was something familiar about you . . . but it was only when you took your hat off and put it on again that I knew where I'd seen you before — "

Ed Killick straightened himself and got rid of a frog in his throat. He still acted like the two of them were alone.

" — before you walked in here. It was that night at Duffie's Hotel. As I went along the hallway to Frankie's room I saw you going towards the top of the stairs."

He still hadn't made a move. I knew what I must do but I didn't relish having to do it.

With triumph in her face, she looked

at me and asked, "Why don't you get him to tell you what he was doing in Frankie's room? Is it because you're in cahoots?"

I said, "He doesn't need to tell me. There's only one way he could've known it was a little bible you found in Frankie's grip. Homicide can fill in the details for themselves."

Ed looked at me over his shoulder with no emotion of any kind in his face. He said, "You're helluva quick at jumping to conclusions. What's happened to all the gratitude you felt when I saved your life?"

I said, "That's what makes me want to throw up. You've condemned yourself out of your own mouth and left me no choice."

"Oh no, I haven't." He tugged a handkerchief out of his breast pocket and wiped it over his face. "The choice is up to you. What's to stop you walking out and forgetting you've ever been here?"

Diane pushed back her dishevelled hair. She said, "He means you should leave him free to give me the same treatment he gave Frankie."

With contempt in her voice, she added, "If you string along he may even cut you in on the Shoemaker diamonds. That would help you forget you were once a guy who kept faith with his clients."

"Only one of us knows what faith means," I said. "You're worse than he is. But don't worry. I'm not walking out."

As Killick wiped his face again, he asked, "Is that your final decision? Is that the thanks I get?"

I said, "If you're adding up the score don't forget that bang on the head you gave me in apartment 412 at Lakeland Towers. And you can also include the scare I got when you shot a hole in my living-room window. That stunt with a ticking clock on the phone is in the debit column as well."

"OK." He shrugged, his not-good-looking-not-ugly face quite impassive. "If that's the way you want it, we're straight . . . "

He looked down at the crumpled handkerchief and then grinned at me as he thrust it into his side pocket.

When his hand came out it was holding a gun.

The case of Frankie Siccola had begun with a .45 automatic. Now it looked like it was going to end the same way. I had let Ed get the drop on me and I had no one to blame but myself.

Diane was more fascinated than scared. I almost admired her for that. Fascination didn't have any share in the way I felt. I was scared — but good.

The grin on Ed Killick's lumpy face wasn't any help, either. He said, "Sorry and all that. Guess we've come to the parting of the ways. Quit holding on to the Smith and Wesson and bring your hand out empty. See you do it nice and slow as well."

I said, "What if I don't?"

"Well, now — " his grin didn't change as he pivoted to face me — "I'd say that was a good question. Of course, you might not like the answer. Want to give it a try?"

"Unless you can suggest an alternative. I might do just that. It won't shorten my prospects by more than a couple of minutes. You can't let me leave here alive."

He put his grin back in mothballs. He said, "That's being pessimistic. Maybe we can come to some arrangement. But first you've got to show willing. So I'm asking you once more for the last time . . . "

It seemed all wrong. This couldn't be real. This couldn't be Ed Killick. Anybody else, but not Ed Killick.

Even the sour old man in my head had nothing to say. But I'll give him credit for one thing — he tried. And while he was trying my attention was concentrated exclusively on Killick's face.

That must've been why I didn't see Diane reach behind her and slide open one of the drawers in the little table. She did it quietly, too. I never heard a sound. And neither did Ed.

First thing I knew she had a gun in her hand — a tiny polished gun that caught the light. First thing Ed knew it went off with a crack like a pencil snapping in two.

Maybe she didn't aim straight. Maybe she meant to hit him in the shoulder.

It didn't matter all that much in the end.

What did matter was that the shell bored into his shoulder like a red-hot knife. He lurched forward and nearly tripped over his own feet while he did his damnedest to hang on to the .45 and make a rightabout turn at the same time.

Guess he'd forgotten about me. That was his big mistake. When he was only half-way round I knocked his gun hand aside, planted a nice solid left in his middle and gave him a right on the point of the chin as he bent double.

He went down like a sack of kindling. And when he hit the floor he lay there.

I let him lie. Diane was looking at him with stupefied eyes as I crossed the space between us and clamped my hand round the shining little gun.

She didn't resist. She was like a woman who'd been drugged. I had better than an idea she'd never used a gun before. When I took it from her she had a bad fit of the shakes that made her teeth chatter.

As I went back and picked up the .45 she was weeping without tears. Her thin despairing voice wailed on and on while I listened to the ringing of the phone bell in Homicide.

14

WHEN all the odds and ends had been cleared up, Henderson said much the same thing as Ed Killick had said " . . . You keep the wrong sort of company."

Guess it was a fair comment. I took an inventory of my life and habits and decided I should make some changes.

For a start I returned Herman Polk's thousand-dollar bribe. That made me feel somewhat better. I wasn't worried about his threats. After Shoemaker Gem Corporation got their diamonds back, Polk wasn't interested in me. He had other fish to fry.

Diane's five-hundred-dollar retainer I kept. I'd earned it. In any case, where she was going she wouldn't need money for quite a while.

Then I did some thinking about Connie — blonde and beautiful Connie. Dumb or not, she was real and she was on the level.

That was more than I could say for Diane Russell. Her kiss had been as sincere as a commercial traveller's handshake.

When I got that far I told myself Connie had been kicked around enough. She deserved a break. And someone like me was no break for someone like her.

So I took a trip out of town and relaxed for two-three weeks. By the time I got back I reckoned she'd have forgotten all about me.

The day I returned was a grim freezing November day that made an old scar ache as I climbed the stairs to my office. Nothing had changed except there was more dust on my desk and the window was even more grubbly than when I'd taken a vacation. The place looked like I felt.

But I'd had that feeling many times before. It always passed. No dose of the gremlins lasted for ever. All I needed was a little stimulus to buck me up.

While I was thinking about it, the phone rang. I knew the caller must be somebody to whom I owed money.

354

It couldn't be anyone else on a day like this.

I was wrong. A woman's voice said, "Gee, it's real nice to hear you again. I've been trying day after day and there was no reply. Where you been all this time?"

There was only one honeysuckle voice like hers. I said, "Why don't you leave well alone? I'm no good for you."

She said, "But you promised. And I don't want you to say things like you're no good. We could have fun, you and me, without any strings. Is that so bad?"

So we talked a while. And at last I couldn't see much sense in arguing any more. But that's another story.

THE END

A FOOT IN THE GRAVE
Bruce Marshall

About to be imprisoned and tortured in Buenos Aires, John Smith escapes, only to become involved in an aeroplane hijacking.

DEAD TROUBLE
Martin Carroll

Trespassing brought Jennifer Denning more than she bargained for. She was totally unprepared for the violence which was to lie in her path.

HOURS TO KILL
Ursula Curtiss

Margaret went to New Mexico to look after her sick sister's rented house and felt a sharp edge of fear when the absent landlady arrived.

THE DEATH OF ABBE DIDIER
Richard Grayson

Inspector Gautier of the Sûreté investigates three crimes which are strangely connected.

NIGHTMARE TIME
Hugh Pentecost

Have the missing major and his wife met with foul play somewhere in the Beaumont Hotel, or is their disappearance a carefully planned step in an act of treason?

BLOOD WILL OUT
Margaret Carr

Why was the manor house so oddly familiar to Elinor Howard? Who would have guessed that a Sunday School outing could lead to murder?

THE DRACULA MURDERS
Philip Daniels

The Horror Ball was interrupted by a spectral figure who warned the merrymakers they were tampering with the unknown.

THE LADIES
OF LAMBTON GREEN
Liza Shepherd

Why did murdered Robin Colquhoun's picture pose such a threat to the ladies of Lambton Green?

CARNABY
AND THE GAOLBREAKERS
Peter N. Walker

Detective Sergeant James Aloysius Carnaby-King is sent to prison as bait. When he joins in an escape he is thrown headfirst into a vicious murder hunt.

MUD IN HIS EYE
Gerald Hammond

The harbourmaster's body is found mangled beneath Major Smyle's yacht. What is the sinister significance of the illicit oysters?

THE SCAVENGERS
Bill Knox

Among the masses of struggling fish in the *Tecta's* nets was a larger, darker, ominously motionless form . . . the body of a skin diver.

DEATH IN ARCADY
Stella Phillips

Detective Inspector Matthew Furnival works unofficially with the local police when a brutal murder takes place in a caravan camp.